A
KILLER
PLOT
A Nosy Neighbor Mystery
Book 2

Cynthia Hickey

Spyglass Lane Mysteries

Discover other Spyglass Lane titles at
SpyglassLaneMysteries.com.
Published in association with MacGregor Literary Inc.,
Portland, Oregon.

Copyright © 2014 Cynthia Hickey
All rights reserved.
ISBN:1500179701
ISBN-13:9781500179700

DEDICATION

To all my fans who have already made this series a success.
It's because of you that I write. Thank you..

ACKNOWLEDGMENTS

To God, for the ideas,
To my husband for his patience,
And to my family who respect my writing time.
Thank you..

1

"How does it feel to be on the NYT Best Seller's list again?" My agent, Elizabeth Swanson, asked.

"Just as wonderful as the first time." Few things were better than seeing my name, Stormi Nelson, on the cover of a book. I sipped my coffee and watched my Irish Wolf Hound, Sadie, chase a squirrel across the yard. After the murders six months ago, and the publication of my first mystery novel, I relished the peace.

"How is your hunky hero?"

"He's been on an undercover assignment for a few months. I'm lucky if I get a phone call from him." Not to mention how much I missed his kisses. After all, I'd designed the hero in my book after him.

"Have you started the next book in the series?"

"I'm waiting for inspiration." Which arrived daily in the form of ever-increasingly disturbing emails. Something I chose to keep to myself at the moment. "I'll keep you updated. Bye."

I hung up, dropped the phone on the table next

to me and studied the email I had received that morning from "Your biggest fan".

"Miss Nelson, I continue to anxiously await your next novel and book signing. Maybe I should help move things along for you? I have certain talents that will help take your mystery writing to the next level. If I don't see a second book soon, I'm afraid I'll have to implement some serious action."

I shuddered. The latest email might not be cause for alarm, if not for all the ones prior. I received one a day from this person, and after answering the first one and letting the sender know it would be well into the next year before a new manuscript would be finished, I'd stopped answering.

"Come on, Sadie." I stood and held the kitchen door open. Sadie bounded inside, almost knocking Mom over in her haste.

"Gracious, that dog is like a bulldozer." Mom set a plate of pancakes on the table. "I wish I had her energy."

"Me, too." I grabbed a pancake, and carrying the disc of fluffy fried batter, headed to my office to start the writing day.

While I ate, I booted up my laptop. Feet pounded down the stairs outside my office. My nephew, Dakota, and niece, Cherokee, were running late for school, as usual. They spent more time in sweep at the high school than they did in class, it seemed. Their mother, Angela, should make sure they're up before she headed to her job as receptionist at the local police station. Still, it wasn't my place to judge.

My laptop came to life and alerted me to another email. The blood drained from my head to my feet as I discovered it was from my biggest fan. Was the person going to email me every hour from now on? I really needed to let Matt know the next time he called. Maybe he could trace the emails somehow and tell the person to lay off.

Speaking of phone calls, I'd left my cell phone outside. Getting out of my chair, I yelled for Mom to bring me the phone when she had a minute. Distractions of one sort or another kept me from actually starting my writing until eight a.m. each morning. That gave me ten more minutes to piddle around until the house quieted down.

"Here you go." Mom pushed open the door and tossed me the phone. "I'm headed out for supplies. A lot of orders to fill."

Mom had started an in-home bakery three months ago and, to my surprise, worked very diligently filling orders. Someday, maybe she could actually have her own bakery and I could have my kitchen back. I felt as if I rarely got to relax by cooking anymore.

"Thank you." I checked for messages from Matt. Nothing. I sighed and settled back into my chair, fingers poised over the keyboard. I needed to write a minimum of three thousand words to stay on track of finishing a rough draft in less than two months.

Two hours and the first chapter done, I was well on my way to a juicy little murder. I'd chosen the crime of, A Killer Plot, to be about an author cyber-stalked by a fanatic fan. A bit close for comfort, considering I'd received two more emails, one an hour, from my very own stalker, but the annoying emails needed to be good for something, right? Why not fodder for a new book? It might be just the thing I needed to avoid an all-out fear fest.

I saved the manuscript and headed to the

kitchen for lunch, sticking my phone in the pocket of my new skinny jeans. Matt hadn't called in over a week. Today might be the day he called and erased my worry about him.

Mom had a rack of cupcakes cooling on the table and filled another pan with batter. "I haven't fixed lunch, yet. Sorry."

"I can fix myself a sandwich. I know you're busy."

"Haven't bought groceries, either."

I sighed. Hadn't she said earlier that she was headed to the store? "No problem. I'll go." I grabbed my purse from next to the refrigerator and grabbed the never-ending list of groceries my family couldn't, or wouldn't, live without. I really needed to start charging people rent.

Once behind the wheel of my Mercedes, I backed out of the driveway and headed to the grocery store. I filled my shopping cart with almost everything on the list, how many candy bars did a teenager need anyway? And got in the long line by the cashier.

"Stormi, it's good to see you." Sarah Thompson, local erotic and horror novel writer, tapped me on the shoulder. "It's been so long, you haven't seen my newest work."

I didn't want to either. The last I'd read had given me nightmares for a week. My neighbor definitely had a twisted mind, and the writing wasn't very good either. "How's the self-publishing business?"

"Booming. There's a real market for steamy stuff. You really should change genres."

I fought back a shudder. "I'm having too much fun to change." My bank account wasn't suffering much either.

"It's a lot more fun to research murder, mayhem, and deviant acts." Sarah wiggled her eyebrows. "Oh, but you're man has been away for a while, hasn't he? You poor thing."

Thankfully, the cashier motioned me forward, saving me from having to answer. At one time, I'd suspected Sarah of being a murderer. After all, she'd said she'd do anything for a story, and her last book had followed the crimes happening in Oak Meadow Estates to a Tee. Still, it had also given me plenty to write about and landed me at number five on the NYT Best Selling list. Write about what you know, right? Since I had been the one to stumble across the first dead body, I'd had plenty of words to put to paper.

"That will be two hundred dollars and thirty-six cents," the cashier said.

I definitely needed to charge my family rent. I pushed my heavy cart back out to the car.

Bill Olsen waved a hand in greeting. His wife, Norma, promptly shoved him away from me and toward the store. The woman's jealousy hadn't dissipated one iota. I grinned. Maybe some women found older, balding, paunchy men attractive, but I was happy with my hunky detective. Now, if he would only call. Matt, not Bill.

Trunk full of food I wouldn't have to buy if I still lived alone, I drove home, unloaded and put away the groceries, and let Sadie into the yard to run. I watched for a few minutes, then filched one of Mom's cupcakes. "Oh, filling!"

Mom glared. "I only made enough extras for each of the family to have one. Don't think you'll get another one tonight when everyone else is enjoying theirs."

"As if Angela would risk the extra calories." I would get my sister's for sure. "Who are these for?"

"The Women's Auxiliary at the church is having a bake sale. They paid me fifty dollars to make two hundred of these to sell." Mom chuckled. "I would have made them for free."

"No sense if they're willing to pay." I took another bite and bit back a moan. "You are a baking genius." Maybe I could help set my mother up in her own shop. I had the money. They could be partners, with me handling the financial aspect.

My pocket vibrated, alerting me to a call. I dug the cell phone out and dashed to the back porch and privacy. "Matt."

"Hey, sweetheart."

"I've missed you." I plopped onto a lawn chair. "When are you coming home?"

"A few more days, I promise. How are things over there?"

I almost told him about my cyber-stalker, but hesitated. He had enough to worry about. "I've started my next book, which will make my agent happy. I could use some research help for the love scenes."

"I'm looking forward to it."

His husky voice sent my pulse racing. "I'm thinking about funding Mom's bakery."

"That's sweet of you."

I grinned. "Her birthday is tomorrow. I'll tell her then. She's amazing, Matt. I've gained five pounds since she started this venture."

"In all the right places, I bet."

"Maybe." And maybe not. My pants had grown a bit snug. I closed my eyes and leaned against the chair back. "Are you staying safe?"

"As much as I'm able. Look, baby, I've got to go. Take care of yourself, okay?"

"You, too." Tears pricked my eyes as I said goodbye and sent up a prayer for his safety. Less than a year ago, I hadn't known he existed, now he filled my heart. Six months was a long time for him to be undercover. Each day, each week, that passed filled me with dread. Each sight of a squad car driving down the street left me cold.

"Hey, Aunt Stormi." Dakota joined me on the porch, handing me a cold diet soda. "Things aren't the same out here without a murder, are they?"

"Don't tell me you're missing a nighttime hike at gunpoint." I popped the soda tab.

"Maybe a little." He grinned and guzzled his soda. "The good thing is it brought us all closer together, don't you think."

I clapped a hand on his knee. "I know it did. I might have grumbled at first when y'all moved in, disrupting my quiet life, but I prefer the occasional bouts of noise." To my surprise, I truly did. Living alone had been a miserable existence. Now, instead of living between the pages of my novels, I actually lived. "Now, to get your sister and you to stop fighting and get to school on time."

"Doubt that will happen." He finished his drink and crushed the can in his hand. "I've got football practice. See you at supper." He bounded away with all the energy of a sixteen-year-old.

I sighed and transferred my attention to Sadie digging under a hydrangea bush. "Sadie, stop that." When the dog ignored me, I pushed off the chair and went to investigate. "I've spent a lot of money on this landscaping, you scoundrel. No digging." I grabbed the dog's collar.

Sadie pulled against my grasp. In the dirt, lay a new rawhide bone, still clean and pristine against the mulch. "Where did that come from?" I picked it up.

"Flowers." Mom called from the house. "Just arrived for you."

Matt! I dashed toward the house, dropping the bone in the garbage on the way.

On the kitchen table sat a bouquet of spring flowers. I grabbed the note and tore open the envelope.

"Does your dog like my gift? Careful. You shouldn't take treats from a stranger."

2

"Call the police." Obviously, I could no longer wait until Matt could handle my email stalker. The lunatic knew where I lived.

"What's wrong?" Mom reached for the wall phone. "Who are the flowers from?"

"A crazy fan." I tossed the note on the table and headed to the living room. After pulling the curtains closed against spying eyes, I fell onto the sofa. Being a romantic mystery writer was far more dangerous than plain romance.

Fifteen minutes later, a navy sedan pulled into the driveway. Two minutes later, the largest black man I'd ever seen slid from behind the steering wheel. His burgundy dress shirt strained over his muscled arms and chest.

"Mercy," Mom said. "That is a big man. Are you ready to tell me what's going on?"

"I'll tell you when I tell him." I opened the front door, not wanting to tell the story once, much less twice.

"I'm Detective Koontz." He shook my hand and almost had to duck to step into the house.

"I expected a regular officer."

He grinned, his teeth startling white against his ebony skin. "Not for Steele's girlfriend. You get the royal treatment."

"I'll make tea. Don't say anything until I get back." Mom rushed to the kitchen.

"Have a seat, Detective. I'll be right back." While Mom bustled around the kitchen, I grabbed the vase of flowers and the note and headed back to the living room. Detective Koontz studied the pictures on the mantel.

"Your sister has made some big changes around the precinct," he said without turning. "Puts flowers on the desks, makes fresh coffee, brings in donuts." He shrugged. "She's spoiling us." He faced me. "But, you like to make us work."

"Give me a little slack. I haven't found any trouble in six months." I set the flowers and note on the coffee table. "You weren't here then, were you?"

"Nah, but I've been filled in." He grinned and squeezed into an easy chair. "I read your book, the fictional one based on what happened here. Interesting."

"Thanks." I sat on the sofa across from him. An uncomfortable silence filled the space as we waited for Mom.

Detective Koontz leaped to his feet when she entered carrying a tray and took it from her, setting it next to the flowers. "All right, then. What's going on?"

"I got these flowers today." I handed him the note. "Maybe not too alarming on its own, but for the last few months, I've been receiving emails from a fan. I don't respond to them, except for the first one, and now they're coming every hour and getting threatening."

"You didn't tell me this!" Mom planted her fists on her hips.

I waved her to sit down. "While it made me nervous, I didn't think too much of it until the flowers came. This nut job knows where I live."

"Do you have the emails?" Koontz's brow furrowed.

"Yes." I rushed to my office and brought him back a handful of print-outs.

He flipped through the pages. "It looks as if you have a stalker. May I take these to our computer guy and see what he can find out?"

"Please, do." I slouched against the back of the sofa. "What do I do in the meantime?"

"Continue on as you are." He stood. "I would advise not going anywhere alone, though. Celebrities don't always have the easiest time of things."

"Here we go again," Mom said. She rubbed her hands together. "Time for the Hickory Hellos to start investigating."

"No, ma'am." Koontz shook his head. "You ladies will stay out of it. We don't want any danger to come to you."

The poor man didn't know my mother. "I have no desire to be at the receiving end of a gun again." I rubbed the scar on my leg. No more short shorts for me.

He shook our hands again, reminded Mom to heed his words, then left. I wanted to ask him what he would charge to be my bodyguard until Matt returned. No one in their right mind would wrestle with Koontz, or Matt for that matter. But Matt wasn't there.

"I bet it's those people who moved into the Edgars' house." Mom peered through a crack in the curtains. "If it is them, I won't be giving them a welcome basket."

The Edgars' had lived next door until everything hit the fan. Then, with them being in the Witness Protection Program, they'd had to move. A new family, a husband and wife, had in last week.

"I don't think my stalker would be dumb enough to move next door." I hugged a throw pillow.

"Ms. Henley had lived right across the street, and you didn't suspect a thing." She gathered up the undrunk tea and headed back to the kitchen.

Good point. I'd suspected her simple-minded son as a killer long before I knew Ms. Henley was responsible for the rash of killings in Oak Meadow Estates. She'd offed several people, all because folks got tired of her son Rusty peeping in people's windows and were going to have him arrested. Miss Marple, I'm not.

"My phone rang. I tossed the pillow out of my lap and grabbed my phone. "Twice in one day, Matt? I'm thrilled."

"Why didn't you tell me you had a stalker?"

Of course Koontz couldn't wait to tell him. Undercover or not, the police had a way of getting a hold of Matt where I couldn't. "I didn't want you to worry. You have enough on your mind."

"Are we in a relationship or not?"

"Well, yes, but—"

"Am I in a position to help you?"

"Usually, but—"

"You should have told me. It hurts that you didn't." He was silent for several long seconds. "Keep

Koontz's number close. He's a good man. I'll call when I can. Love you." Click.

Ugh. Now, I felt like a horrible person. Sometimes, you just couldn't win. What if Matt got into a dangerous situation and lost concentration because of worrying about me and something happened to him? I'd never be able to live with myself.

"What do we do now?" Mama perched on the edge of the seat Koontz had vacated.

"There isn't anything we can do." I set my phone on the table. "I know you're itching to start gum-shoeing again, but we've nothing to go on." Besides, I couldn't erase the horror of the last time we tried our hand at crime solving. I wasn't eager to put myself, or my family, into that type of situation again.

"Pity."

"Don't you have enough to do with your baking?"

"Sure, but a little detecting during down time wouldn't hurt."

"It could kill us." I pushed to my feet. "I'm taking Sadie for a walk."

The moment I slipped the leash from the hook beside the back door, Sadie came running. She leaned up on me, bringing her face even with mine. "Yes, we're going." I laughed and clipped the leash to her collar. Despite the circumstances of finding the body of Sadie's former owner, I counted myself blessed to have such a loyal friend. I chuckled at remembering how the dog and I had hid in a dog house together, both too afraid to come out and face the attacker.

Without glancing toward the Henley house, which still stood vacant, I headed down the street. My new next door neighbors puttered in their backyard, stopping as Sadie and I got close. I tossed them a smile and a wave and started past.

"Good evening." A tall statuesque brunette got off her knees beside a flower bed and came toward me. A man, only a couple of inches taller than his wife, turned off the lawnmower.

"Good evening," I replied, trying not to sneeze at the tickle of freshly mown grass.

"I'm Diane Wood." She peeled off a pair of pink gardening gloves. "That handsome man is my husband, Mark. What kind of dog is that? It's huge."

"This is Sadie, my Irish Wolf Hound. Don't worry about her size. She's a big baby." Sadie leaned against me.

"You're the author, right? Stormi Nelson?" She grinned, showing professionally whitened teeth. "I've read all your books, even the murder one. That's what attracted us to this house. I feel as if I already know all the neighbors, despite you changing their names."

I kept a smile plastered to my face, despite the new chatty Cathy, who I feared would be a regular disruption to my life. "Thank you. Well, we're off on our walk."

"Okay. We'll find time later for a good long chat."

I felt her gaze on my back until I turned the corner. Please, God, don't let my new neighbor be the stalker. At least not an evil one. I'd dealt with avid readers before, they didn't worry me. It was those who came at me without showing their face that set spiders skittering up and down my spine.

A car pulled alongside me. I turned to see Detective Koontz grinning from behind the wheel. "Should you be out alone? It's getting dark."

"I'm not alone. I have my dog." But not my phone or the gun and mace Mom had bought me months ago. "Did Matt tell you to keep an eye on me?"

"Yes, ma'am." He turned off the ignition and exited the car. "Mind if I walk with you?"

I shrugged. "It's your feet that will be blistered in those dress shoes."

He laughed. "I can handle it."

His shoes beat out a steady clip-clop to my gym shoes' softened slap. I could tell something was on the man's mind, but decided to wait until he was ready to talk again. We strolled through the gates leading into the community and turned right. When we approached the coffee shop, he stopped.

"Mind if we sit? I'll get us both something to drink. What will you have?"

"The biggest mocha flavored drink they have." I pulled out a wrought-iron bistro style chair and sat, looping Sadie's leash around the table leg. We didn't usually venture out of the gated community on our walks, but if it would take time for Koontz to talk, I wanted to give it to him.

The long-ago, once busy, Main Street sported a women's boutique, floral shop, drug store, ice cream parlor, and Ma and Pop convenience store. Too many of the storefront windows were blank. It was easy to envision Mom's bakery filling one of them. Her store would be one more step toward Main Street becoming the gathering place it had once been.

Ordering Sadie to stay, I peered into the dark window next to the ice cream shop. Empty display stands filled the front half, while work tables occupied the back. I couldn't see much more than that, but it looked perfect. I noted the number on the window to

15

memory and returned to the table where Koontz sat watching me.

"Okay, you can spill the beans now." I sat and sipped my drink.

"The IP address where the emails came from belongs to this coffee shop."

Smart man. While I'd thought I was leading him, he was steering me right to where he wanted me. I glanced toward the shop's door. "You work fast."

"Matt asked us to rush it. Problem is … we have no way of knowing whether it's one of the employees, or a customer, sending the emails." He removed the lid to his cup and added cream.

The delightful scent of roasted coffee beans pleased my senses.

He caught me watching, and shrugged. "I like a little coffee with my cream."

I laughed. "That's why I stick to the froo-froo drinks. I love the smell, but the taste is too bitter." I twirled my straw in my drink. "Where do we go from here?"

His dark eyes met mine. "You be careful where you go and who you're with until we catch this guy. Most stalkers aren't dangerous, physically, but once in a while—"

"You find one who goes off the deep end."

3

The next morning, despite Koontz's warning, I took my laptop to the coffee shop and settled down to write. I figured not much harm could come to me in a crowded place, right? This gave me the opportunity to scope out the other customers. I pretended to be involved in my work, while in all actuality, I continuously peered over my laptop and spied on the other customers.

A young man typed furiously on a tablet, an elderly couple conversed while sipping coffee and eating pastries, while others simply sat and read. Quiet murmurs drifted from the other tables as patrons took advantage of free wifi and great coffee. Not a single person looked like a dangerous stalker to me.

The male Barista appeared kind of creepy with dyed black hair under a hair net, more piercings than I had fingers on one hand, and dark eyeliner, but that wouldn't necessarily mean he cared about how quickly I wrote my next book. Although, he would make an interesting secondary character.

I ducked back behind my screen when Sarah

Thompson strolled in. *Don't let her see me, don't let her see me* … she plopped onto the seat opposite me.

"Hello."

I took my lower lip between my teeth and did my best not to grimace. "Hello."

"I didn't think you came here to write." She set a laptop on the table and opened it. "What fun. We can write together."

Oh, goody. "I can't really write with distractions. I'm actually here to observe."

"The perfect place." She grinned. "I come here all the time. The barrister, Tyler, he's actually in my book. I changed his name, of course, but he has an unhealthy obsession with one of my characters. Then there's a young girl who sometimes comes in here, and she's got a secret crush on him. In my book, of course. The story is all about her sexual fantasies. Brilliant, right?"

I shuddered. Since I didn't know what to say, I chose to keep my thoughts to myself, although I was dying to ask her how she planned on researching her current story. The woman's imagination was eerie and horrifying. The answer might scare me into next week.

"What are you working on?" Sarah asked.

"My next mystery."

"Oooh, are you looking for a killer here?" She turned in her seat.

If she only knew. "I'm only studying body language and such right now." Too bad she couldn't read mine. It was screaming for her to leave. "I need to use the restroom."

"Go ahead. I'll watch your purse. You can trust just about anyone in here." She waved a hand signaling for me to go.

Despite my reservations, I went. I had nothing in the purse that couldn't be replaced with a few phone calls, and I rarely carried more than twenty dollars in cash. When I'd completed my business, I headed back to the table, surprised to see Sarah at the front of the store conversing with a young girl in too short of shorts and a barely-there top.

I grabbed my purse and checked my watch. Ten o'clock. Time to head across the street and see about renting the vacant storefront for Mom. "It was nice chatting with you, but I've an errand to run," I called, closing my laptop. I slid it into its quilted bag. "Happy writing." I flashed what I hoped was a grin rather than a grimace, and got out of there as fast as I could.

Maybe it was wrong of me, but I didn't want readers to think I wrote in the same, sick, twisted genre she did. My books might contain a little steam, but they were clean for the most part. Something I prided myself on. Anyone could write smut, it took a real author to create sexual tension without the reader having to endure all the private details.

I stood outside the empty store and dialed the number on the sign.

"Weston Realty, this is Jane speaking."

"Hi, Jane. I'm interested in the property located at 302 Main Street. Could you tell me how much it rents for?"

"It's actually not for rent. It's a commercial sale priced at one hundred thousand dollars."

Ouch. I could afford it, but it would take a big chunk of my savings. "I'm standing outside of it now. Could you possibly meet me here?"

"I'll be there in ten minutes." Click.

In eight minutes, a platinum blond, her red suit

straining over ample curves, tottered toward me on stilettos. Her ruby-red lips parted in a grin. "I'm so happy to see someone interested. It's a shame so many places on this street are empty, but one-by-one, we're selling them." She dug a massive key ring from her purse and unlocked the door. "I'm Jane Winston."

"Stormi Nelson." I followed her inside. It was just as it looked from outside except for a small bathroom tucked into a corner and a slightly larger storage room opposite it. "I'll take it. Can I write a check?"

Her eyes bugged. "You want it now? Oh, wait, you're the author."

I smiled. "I'm purchasing this for my mother. Is the seller willing to pay for any renovations?"

"I'm afraid not. The previous owner died years ago." She pulled my mystery book out of her purse. "Will you sign this for me? I'm halfway finished and loving every word. For you, I'll drop the price to ninety-thousand. It actually belonged to my uncle."

"Thank you." I signed my name on the cover page with a flourish and dug in my bag for the checkbook. Mom would be so thrilled.

A few minutes later, I headed home with a receipt in my purse. The official title of ownership would arrive in the mail in a few days. I could hardly wait to see Mom's face that evening when we had cake and presented our gifts.

I spent the rest of the day in my office writing while Mom spent the day with her friends from church. I'd left her a note earlier saying Happy Birthday, but had yet to lay eyes on her that day. Her or any other member of my family. Ebony and Ivory, my cats, slept on the windowsill and Sadie curled up next to my feet.

At least they provided a bit of company. I'd grown used to some kind of noise around me since my family moved in, and found writing in complete silence more difficult than before.

I sighed and tried to focus. My email stalker—real and the fictional one from my story—weren't talking to me either.

The sound of the front door closing had me out of my seat and running down the hall. "Happy Birthday."

"Thanks." Angela set her purse on the foyer table and opened a shopping bag from an elite bakery store. "But it isn't my birthday."

"I thought you were Mom."

"I'm home early to decorate for her party."

"We're having a party?"

She shrugged. "Just the family, but everyone appreciates a little extra effort now and again. What did you get Mom? I bought her a set of expensive cake decorating tools."

I gulped. Angela would get in a snit when she found out I'd bought Mom a store. "I, uh, bought her a vacant storefront."

"What?!" She slammed her purchase on the table. "Why do you have to show the rest of us up? Just because you have all this money, doesn't mean you have to flaunt it. Look at your house."

"You mean the one you're living in rent free?" I cocked my head. "It seems as if everyone is benefiting from my money."

"I can't talk to you." She stormed into the kitchen.

"What's really wrong with you?" I reached into the refrigerator and pulled out the steaks I had marinating for that night's dinner. "You're grouchier than usual."

Angela sniffed, cracking eggs into a bowl. "Wayne broke up with me. He said it was too ... conflicting to work with his girlfriend."

"Oh, honey." I dropped the steaks on the stove and wrapped my arms around her. "He's an idiot."

"I know. I'm such a catch. I'm thirty-two years old with two teenage kids, both of whom were born before I was out of high school and shortly after." She shook her head then wiped her arm across her eyes. "I'm every man's dream."

"You are." I gave her a little shake. "Your children are almost grown. If you find the right man, you're still young enough to have more children if you want. A good man won't hold your past against you."

"Of course you would say that. You're Miss Perfect." She reached for a box of cake mix. "I don't even know how to bake well enough to make Mom's cake from scratch."

"Neither do I." I needed to get the steaks ready, but felt bad about leaving my sister alone while in distress about her boyfriend dumping her. I did the only thing I could think of to do that might take her mind off her own problems. "I have an internet stalker."

"See?" She whirled, waving a wooden spoon that dripped chocolate cake batter. "Your life is so much more interesting than mine."

"Uh, don't you remember how we almost died six months ago? Do you seriously consider a stalker something you envy?"

She quirked her mouth. "Not really. It's just that, there's always something going on with you. I bet Mom is thrilled to have another mystery to solve.

Something the two of you can do together."

Excluding her, she meant. "I have no intentions of solving this on my own. But, if I do, you're more than welcome to join me."

"Really?" Her eyes lit up. "What have you got?"

I sighed. "Some weirdo is mad because I don't have the second mystery book written yet. They've said they will help me along in creative ways. They dropped a bone in the backyard for Sadie, and sent me flowers. I called the police, and they traced the internet connection to the coffee shop."

"That's it? It isn't much."

"That's it." Unfortunately, I feared there would be more clues in the name of research coming. I glanced at the clock. "We're late. Mom is going to be home any minute and the cake isn't even in the oven."

"Crikey." She slid the pan into the oven and set the temperature and timer. "What do you think? One extra minute since it isn't pre-heated?"

"Sure." I stepped onto the patio, missing Matt more than ever. Usually, when I wanted something grilled, I invited him to dinner and he did the honors. Then, after we ate, we'd sit on the back porch and do some necking which was better than any dessert ever created. Plus, I was pretty sure since we heated up the place, we most likely burned calories at the same time.

I grinned and pressed the ignite button. Whoosh! Flames shot up, singing my eyebrows and setting my bangs on fire. I screamed and slapped at the embers that ruined what was once a stylish hair style.

"Is that a new dance move?" Angela called out the window.

"No! I set my hair on fire."

The door opened and a glass of ice water

landed on my head, glass and all. "Ow!"

"You said you were on fire." Angela planted her fists on her hips.

"You aren't supposed to throw the glass, too!" I tenderly touched my smarting forehead. "How bad is it?"

"Um." She bit her bottom lip to keep from laughing. "Not too bad."

"You're lying." I pushed past her and into the downstairs powder room. "Oh, no." Nothing but stubble sat on my head two inches back from my normal hairline. "I have a book signing this weekend."

Angela laughed and leaned against the doorframe. "Guess you'll have to learn stylish ways of wearing a head scarf."

"Shut up." Tears pricked my eyes. I sniffed. Was that burnt plastic smell coming from my head? Maybe, but I smelled something else, too. "Do you smell that?"

"Yeah, it's your head."

"No, something else."

"My cake!" She turned and dashed back to the kitchen.

By the time I got there, she'd pulled out the cake pan. In the center of the pan was the wooden spoon, blackened on the handle from where it had rested against the oven's heat source. "So much for the cake."

"Go buy one from the store." Angela tossed it in the garbage.

"Not looking like this, I won't."

"Looking like what?"

I turned and stared into the smiling face of Matt.

4

"You're home." I launched myself into his arms.

He held me close and, ignoring my sister who stared as if she'd never seen a kiss before, claimed my lips with his own, teasing and tugging, his tongue lightly flicking against mine, until I thought my legs would give out. Then, when I thought I needed to pull away in order to breathe, he pulled me closer, deepening the kiss.

Hearts pounding, chests heaving, he held me at arm's length. "Now, that's a welcome home." He frowned. "What happened to your hair?" He tapped the shaggy edges of what used to be my bangs.

"The grill kind of exploded." I touched the tender spot on my higher than usual forehead. I probably should have examined the burn and put aloe vera on it right away.

"It looks like it hurts."

"It does." I pulled my hair from one side to the other in an attempt to hide the damage. I was sure it didn't look near as sexy swept to the side as I wanted it to.

"Did you have the gas on for too long before igniting?" He glanced out the window.

"It's possible." I'd been arguing with my sister, after all.

"Why are you wet?"

"I tried to put out the fire," Angela said. "It worked, too. Keep your hair swept over like that," she directed to me. "Maybe Mom won't notice."

Her attack with the water hadn't really helped. I'd pounded the sizzling strands with my bare hands, watching charred pieces of my hair fall to the ground before the water glass ever hit me in the head. But, I was too happy at Matt's sudden return to argue. "Why didn't you call?"

"I wanted to surprise you." He put an arm around my shoulders and directed me back to the grill where he had steaks broiling within minutes. "We'll discuss the internet happenings after supper, okay?"

Of course he hadn't forgotten, even in the throes of steamy kisses. I sat in a lawn chair and studied him to my heart's content. Tall, muscular, with hair the color of burnished wheat I'd seen in the fields of Oklahoma once, and eyes the color of coffee, he was the epitome of a handsome hunk. Fortunately, the inside was as attractive as the outside. Matt was a true man through and through, and I was thrilled to have him back in one piece. I sent a prayer of thanks heavenward

"Stormi is staring at your butt," Angela said, handing each of us a can of soda. "She's checking you out big time."

"That's okay." Matt grinned and winked. "I stare at her's all the time."

Angela made a face and stormed back into the kitchen, muttering something about having to go buy a cake.

"Wayne broke up with her today," I explained, popping the tab on the top of my can. "She's a bit disgruntled. He said it was too difficult to date someone he was working with."

Matt flipped the fillets with a long pronged fork. "I'm sorry to hear that. I really thought he liked her. Maybe I can fish around for information when I go to work in the morning." He glanced over his shoulder. "Tonight, it's all about you and me."

"Actually, it's my mother's birthday. That's why we're having the steaks."

"You told me yesterday. I forgot." His eyes widened. "I've butted in. I should go."

"Not a chance. Mom adores you. Please stay."

He set the fork down and leaned over me, his hands balanced on each of the chair's arms. His eyes stared into mine. "Is she the only one who adores me?"

"I'm sure we could find one or two other people." I grinned. "If we looked really hard."

"That's all?" He brought his mouth closer to mine. "Maybe with some convincing—"

"Matthew!" Mom stepped onto the back porch. "You're back."

He shrugged and straightened, gathering Mom close and landing a kiss on her cheek. "Safe and sound. Happy Birthday."

"Stormi has been like a grizzly bear since you've been gone."

"I do tend to sooth the savage in her," Matt said.

He provoked the beast, more than soothed. His

27

kisses spiked my blood pressure, got my heart to racing, and left me weak. He was more like a disease that I didn't want to get over. "You two are hilarious." I took a big gulp of my soda.

Matt and Mom chattered while he grilled the steaks, and I focused on the emails I'd been receiving. Not to mention the gifts my stalker had sent. Matt was going to blow hotter than the grill when I told him the details. From the way he kept glancing at me over Mom's shoulder, told me he suspected I would try to find a way to sugarcoat the details. I sighed and took another drink, idly twirling Sadie's hair around my finger.

By the time the steaks were done, I'd worked myself into a tangled knot of nerves. I held open the kitchen door while Matt carried the steaks inside. On the counter sat some kind of whipped cream and strawberry concoction which supposedly was Mom's birthday cake. She eyed it with suspicion, glanced at Angela, then shrugged and took her seat at the head of the table.

Angela had salad and baked potatoes with all the fixings ready for the family to dig in. Cherokee and Dakota practically salivated as Matt dropped steaks on their plates. I sat to the right of the opposite end of the table where Matt always sat when he came over for dinner, which was quite often when he wasn't away working.

"Sorry, I'm late." Mary Ann, Matt's sister and my best friend sailed into the room.

"You're right on time," Mom said.

Mary Ann plopped into the chair on Matt's left. "Perfect. Oh, this all looks so good. I'm glad to see you back safe, big brother. Sorry I wasn't home when you got there."

"I came straight here." He winked at me.

Pleasure that my house was his first stop flooded through me and plastered a goofy grin to my face.

"Matt, lead us in the blessing, please," Mom said.

We held hands around the table while Matt blessed the food and asked for a special blessing on Mom for her birthday. A chorus of "amens" rang out before everyone started passing the plates around.

"Can you tell us anything about the case you were working on?" Mom asked, glancing at Matt. "You know how this family enjoys a mystery."

"Nope. Not unless I want to jeopardize my undercover alias." He speared a hunk of meat with his fork. "After the trial, I might be able to spill a few of the details, but my safety and the safety of everyone I care about could be in danger if I say too much."

"Speaking of too much … " Mom wiggled her eyebrows at me. "Stormi has a secret admirer."

"Of course she does." Angela tossed her napkin on the table. "Everything is always bright in Stormi's world."

"Mom," I warned. "You know it isn't an admirer, and I don't want to discuss it at the table."

"Is someone trying to kill you again?" Dakota set his glass down and leaned forward, fixing his gaze on me. "Because that was easily the most exciting time of my life."

"Right, like fifteen is living a long life." Cherokee dropped a dollop of sour cream on her potato. "It was my knowing the area that kept us from being killed."

Wow, I had no idea that the troubles I got

myself into were a competition between my niece and nephew. I met Matt's serious gaze, and focused back on my plate. The more my family carried on, the less I would be able to downplay the seriousness of the emails I'd received. It wasn't that I thought them inconsequential, I didn't. I realized the severity of having a psycho stalker. I just didn't want Matt to flip out and keep me a prisoner in my own home. Maybe I could rent a mountain cabin somewhere and hide out until I finished writing my book.

We finished eating, cleaned up from supper, and then set the cake, complete with fifty-two candles, in front of Mom's seat. She laughed, warning us we'd set off the smoke alarms if she didn't blow out the candles soon. We sang Happy Birthday, then she blew, extinguishing all fifty-two in one breath. She clapped. "Presents."

Angela retrieved a bright pink bag from the counter, glaring at me while I fetched the manila envelope with Mom's store information. Cheyenne and Dakota gave Mom a box with a necklace with two jeweled children figures; one with each of their birthstones.

"I love it." She slipped the necklace over her head.

"Here's mine." Angela forced a smile to her face, despite the tenseness to her tone.

"Oh, sweetie." Mom pulled out a kit for decorating cakes. "This will get a lot of use. Thank you."

"Happy Birthday, Mom." I handed her my gift.

She lifted the flap and pulled out the sheets of paper. "What's this?"

"I bought you a store front on Main Street. Now, you can expand your business." My face hurt from

30

grinning. "You're a business owner now."

Tears welled in her eyes. "I never thought I'd own my own business." She glanced at each of us in turn. "Summer jobs for you kiddos and the perfect opportunity to use my new tools … I must be the most blessed woman in Oak Meadows."

Angela's frown turned to a smile when she realized Mom considered her gift as important as mine. In true mother form, Mom didn't favor one child's gift over another.

"All you need now is a name, obtain a license, and fill the place with good smells and awesome baked delicacies," Mary Ann said. "You should do well. There isn't another bakery in a twenty-mile radius."

"I don't even know where to begin." Mom stared at the papers in her hand.

"How about you begin by looking the place over in the morning?" I patted her on the shoulder. "It's Saturday. We'll make it a family affair." I dug the store keys out of my pocket and handed them to her.

"That's a wonderful idea." She wiped her eyes on her sleeve, then focused on me. "What happened to your hair? Is that a burn? Were you attacked?" She lunged to her feet.

"No, Mom, just an accident with the grill."

"I've told you that cantankerous thing needs a man's touch to work properly."

I shrugged, thinking of how every woman under my roof could use a man's touch, then nodded to Matt that I was ready to talk and led the way to the front porch where we took our seats on the swing. I wanted to clutch a throw pillow to my chest, but the gesture would only serve to make me look defensive.

He put his arm around my shoulders, but before

he could pull me close, I stiffened and dug copies of the emails out of the pocket of my jeans. "I didn't think anything about these at first, as I told you on the phone, but they're getting increasingly hostile. Not to mention the dog bone I found in the yard and the flowers that were delivered. Koontz has suggested I not go anywhere alone."

"That's a great idea." A muscle ticked in Matt's jaw.

"No, it isn't." I faced him. "If I make my family go with me everywhere, I'm putting them in the same danger they were in six months ago. I can't do that to them again."

"I understand." He shoved the paper in his pocket. "I'm not crazy about this happening to you again, either." He sighed. "Once upon a time, I thought that getting into a relationship with a woman would endanger her because of my profession, not hers. Now, I realize how egotistical that was. You don't need me to get into danger. It follows you like a noxious cloud."

"It's not something I did on purpose. I should have stuck to writing plain romance. It was a lot safer." I snuggled against him. "But, if I back out of the mysteries now, my agent will kill me, not to mention my stalker. Sorry, bad choice of words. Plus, I made a boatload of money on that first mystery and really want to make a series."

"But do you have to write about true events? You're a fiction writer. Make stuff up."

"It's a bit late for that now." The only thing I could do at this point was write the book being handed to me on a silver platter and try to stay alive as I wrote it.

5

The next morning, minus Matt and Mary Ann, we all stood in front of Mom's shop, armed with cleaning supplies, and watched her cry. The hand holding the keys shook like an old Chihuahua. "Do you want me to open the door for you?" I asked.

She shook her head. "I'm just so overwhelmed with gratitude. God is so good." She finally got the key inserted in the lock and the door opened. "After today, I'll go through the back door, like a real owner." Shoulders back, chest puffed out, Mom led the way into her home away from home.

"You weren't kidding when you said the place needed a good cleaning." Mom plopped her fists on her hips. "We'll sweep and dust first, then those shelves on the wall will need to be painted. I can't put baked goods on them, but I can sell baking paraphernalia. Oh, the wheels are turning now." She grinned. "Those glass fronted cases are perfect for smaller baked goods and a few ready-made cakes. The others, I'll make and take pictures of so I have a catalog. Dakota, I'd like you to set me up with a website. Can you do that?"

"Sure, just as soon as you buy a computer." He propped a broom against the wall. "Why don't we head to the electronics store while the others clean?"

The sneaky little devil. I knew exactly what he was trying to do, and it was actually a good plan. We'd never get the place clean with Mom barking orders. Before we'd finished one project, she'd be bound to add several more. "We'll have this place in tip-top shape before you can say, 'Stormi writes great books'." I smiled.

Angela rolled her eyes and stormed toward the back of the store. As much as I enjoyed teasing her, it was time to ease off. What could I do to uplift her spirits? It couldn't relate to money, that would set her off for sure. Maybe a visit to the police station to have a little chat with Wayne and find out exactly why he dumped my beautiful sister. It had to be more than the fact they worked together. A receptionist and a detective didn't have a lot of work time to associate, did they?

"Can you grab us some coffees?" Cherokee asked. "The caffeine might help us work."

"That's a great idea." I set down the bucket full of supplies. "I'll be back as soon as possible. Try to cheer your Mom up, okay? Maybe you two can come up with a name for the bakery, and not Nelson's Bakery. That's boring."

She nodded and headed toward the back where all the magic of Mom's baking would happen in a few weeks. I pushed open the door, glancing above me. A bell would be nice to alert Mom when someone entered and she was busy in the back. Outside, I glanced both ways before crossing the street.

Two doors down, a figure in a trench coat and hat stared into the window of a bookstore. Maybe I wouldn't have taken a second glance had we been in the throes of winter, but since we were only in early October, the coat and hat seemed like overkill. Maybe it was a secret spy lurking in town to find a terrorist. I chuckled at my over-active imagination and dashed across the street and into the coffee shop.

I thought weekday mornings were busy. The line was almost out the door and every table was filled with readers and those working on laptops. Tyler, the young man Sarah was modeling her hero after, was hopping to fill drink orders. I glanced around those in front of me and studied his inky black hair tied back in a ponytail and his multiple piercings. I couldn't see how the boy fit anyone's description of a hero, at least not for an adult novel. Maybe he could do something heroic in a Young Adult book, though.

I glanced around while the line inched forward. Sarah sat hunkered over her laptop in the corner. I angled away from her, praying she wouldn't see me. Jane Weston, the realtor, brushed past me, a carrier full of coffee balanced in one hand while she talked on her cell phone. She flashed me a grin, mouthed the words 'call me', and pushed backward through the door. Since I'd exhausted spotting anyone else I knew, I studied my fingernails and noted how badly I could use a manicure. My mind instantly drifted toward the emails.

Since I hadn't wanted to ruin my morning, I hadn't checked yet that day, and the not knowing was eating at my stomach like an ulcer. The not knowing was almost as bad as reading the hateful words.

"Please don't tell me you're out alone." Koontz's words next to my ear almost had me fall into a faint.

I turned. "My family is right across the street. Besides, this place is as crowded as a sardine can. Are you following me?"

He jabbed me in the side with an ink pen. "See how easy that was? Even here? What if it had been a knife?"

Seriously. "Then, Matt would be angry at both of us. Go away."

"I'm buying a drink."

I decided to ignore him and planned the conversation I'd have with Matt when I got home. I did not need a babysitter.

Five mocha flavored frozen coffees later, I stepped back outside and blinked against the early autumn sun. The long-sleeved tee-shirt I'd put on that morning kept the chill at bay. I smiled, ready to tackle the cleaning.

From the alley next to Mom's shop, stepped the overly dressed spy. Catching a glimpse of the person once was okay, but twice seemed a bit suspicious. I stood there like an idiot until Koontz stepped beside me.

"What's up?" he asked. "Do you need someone to help you cross the street?" His teeth flashed against his dark skin. "Want me to carry those for you?"

The coated figure darted out of sight. "No, I thought I saw someone I knew, that's all. Have a good day." I stepped off the sidewalk and made my way carefully to the other side. Someone had propped the shop door open, making it easy for me to step inside. I decided to play Scarlett O'Hara and worry about the stranger tomorrow.

Angela and Cherokee had the shelves wiped off

and the floor swept by the time I came in. I headed to the back and set the coffees on a battered metal desk pushed against one wall. I could easily envision Mom seated there taking orders by web or by phone.

Oh, no. I'd been so excited to give her a store of her own, I hadn't thought of other expenses. She would need a commercial grade oven, more than one, actually, and a large refrigerator. I sighed. Maybe I could become a partner and at least have the appliances reimbursed, or I could cosign for a business loan.

"Thanks for the coffee." Angela propped one hip on the corner of the desk and grabbed a cup. "Why the long face?"

"Trying to figure out the easiest way to stock the store."

"Mom can get a loan."

"That's what I was thinking." I leaned on the wall opposite my sister and sipped my drink. "Maybe Mom could borrow extra, and you could work for her? Then, maybe Wayne would reconsider since you wouldn't be working at the precinct."

"I heard he already has a new girlfriend. She's the new 9-1-1 operator."

"Do you know that for sure?"

"That she's new?"

"No, that he's dating her?"

Angela shrugged. "She told me. We've gotten pretty close after the whole fiasco six months ago. Now, I don't want anything more from her than to throttle her."

"What's her name?"

"Cheryl Isaacson." Angela made a face. "I gave her a piece of my mind, and while it didn't have Wayne calling me, I did feel better."

Hmmm. I would definitely be talking to Wayne and this Cheryl person. I might be the younger sister, but I'd always been the defender. No one treats my sister this way except me.

"We've got the computer," Dakota called out, lugging a box into the store. "And a phone, and a copier/fax machine. I think Grandma bought out the place."

"I did not. I opened a line of credit for the store. It's all tax deductible." Mom carried in a smaller box and set it on the counter.

"We'll need to visit the bank," I said. "You'll need a loan for the appliances and whatever else you need to start up your business."

"I'll make a list tonight and start pricing things so we know how much." Mom rubbed her hands together. "I'm hoping to open by the end of the month. Is that too early? I don't want to miss the holiday rush. I'm going to call my place, Heavenly Bakes."

"That's cute." I added business license to our list of things to acquire. "I'm not sure we can be up and running by the end of the month, but probably in time for the Christmas season." Although, if Mom had her way, she'd open right when she wanted to, one way or the other.

Mom handed Dakota a coffee and took the last one for herself. "We'll have this place cleaned up today, I'll make a list and price things tonight, and we'll hit the bank and get the license Monday morning. Dakota, get started on my website. Angela, I have a box of pictures of the special cakes and cookies I've made for people. I'll need your help going through those for the best quality ones. This will work. I know it will."

I hoped so. I felt sorry for anyone who got in

Mom's way when she was determined to have something done in a certain amount of time. I set my coffee aside and grabbed a rag. The store wouldn't clean itself and I could get started on the display cases. Dakota got busy hooking up the electronics.

The day passed in a flurry of activity. By supper time, we were tired and cranky, but looking with satisfaction at a clean store. "Mom, until your appliances are ordered you could start your business on a smaller scale and continue baking at home and selling from here."

"What a great idea! Cherokee, I need a sign for the window. Something big, bright, and beautiful. We open for business on Wednesday." Mom grabbed her purse and sailed out the door.

I glanced at Angela, who shrugged and ushered her children out the door. With a final look around the place, I closed the door so Mom could lock up. I had a spare, but would leave all the details to her. I had enough to occupy my mind.

Back at home, I booted up my computer and headed for the shower. Ten minutes later, clean and in my pajamas, I planted myself in my office chair and pulled up my emails. One from my agent who let me know I was still on the New York Times Bestselling list, and one from my stalker. I opened the email.

"Famous romance authors shouldn't be running around town in unattractive clothes or dirtying their hands cleaning. How will you get your next book written? What if someone saw you looking like a scullery maid? Tsk tsk, Stormi. I'm disappointed in you. You need to take me seriously. The punishment for disobedience can be rather severe."

6

I stood outside the police station and glanced at my watch. In one hour, I had to meet Mom at the bank to see about a business loan. For now, I mentally prepared myself to speak with Wayne Jones before my sister showed up for work in half an hour. I was cutting things too close for comfort. If discovered, Angela would skin me and hang my hide from the police station's flag pole.

Taking a deep breath, I pushed open the door and stepped up to the reception desk. Since it was only eight thirty in the morning, all that greeted me was a small metal bell. I slapped it and waited for someone to notice me.

Luck was with me. Wayne Jones came from a back room. He scowled when he saw me. "Stormi."

"Wayne." I forced a grin. "Is there somewhere we can talk privately?"

"An interrogation room?"

"Be nice. I was thinking of inviting you for coffee." I rolled my eyes.

"I can always do coffee." He called back to

someone that he'd be back in a bit and followed me to my car. "I thought you had a Mercedes?"

I shrugged. "Traded it in for a Prius yesterday. Better gas mileage."

"The Mercedes is classier."

I never could figure out what my sister liked about the big, dumb, football player types. I preferred my men muscular, sleek like a panther, and smart.

I pulled up to the drive-thru window of the coffee shop and ignored Wayne's curious glance. It wasn't like we could go inside and spend time together without everyone in Oak Meadows making up rumors. No, I planned on taking him back to the police station and parking behind the building. The coffee was to sweeten the mood.

By the time we arrived back at the station, Wayne's square face was set in hard lines. "What's this all about?"

"Well," I sipped my blended mocha drink. "I'm curious as to why you broke up with my sister."

"Seriously?" He angled his body toward me. "Isn't Angela old enough to fight her own battles?"

"I'm just curious, especially since rumor has it that you're dating Cheryl Isaacson."

"Hardly. I've decided not to date women I work with."

"You don't work with Cheryl, not really, and how often do you really have to speak with the receptionist?" I cocked my head. "I know it isn't any of my business, but Angela is broken up about it. I'm only making sure you are treating her right and letting a bit of time go by before jumping into the pool again."

"You writers and your metaphors." He shook his head. "I'm not dating anyone at this time. I have no idea where the rumors got started about me and Cheryl. I can't stand the woman." He shoved open the car door. "Now, I've got a job to do. Go meddle in someone else's love life. Don't you have another book to write?"

Fine. The big jerk. Maybe I was being a bit nosey and sticking my nose where it didn't belong, but Angela is much easier to live with when she's happy. I got out of the car and strolled to the smaller building next door to the police station which housed the 9-1-1 operators. I spotted Angela getting out of her car as I passed between the buildings. I'd left Wayne just in time.

"Oh. My. Gosh!" A woman so thin that if she stood sideways and stuck out her tongue she'd look like a zipper, bolted to her feet and dashed around the counter. "It's Stormi Nelson."

"Uh, hello." I bit the inside of my bottom lip. The woman's exuberance frightened me and I couldn't breathe when she wrapped her arms around my neck. Her perfume smelled as overpowering as diesel fuel at a truck stop.

"I'm your biggest fan, I swear I am." She pulled back, placing a hand on each of my shoulders and peering into my face. "I'm Cheryl Isaacson. I am so glad to meet you."

Oh, boy. The phone ringing behind her rescued me as Cheryl dashed to take the call since the other two operators were busy. From her side of the conversation, it appeared as if someone had fallen out of a tree. I said a quick prayer for their safety and settled on a hard plastic chair to wait, rethinking my original reason for arriving.

I couldn't very well say, "Are you dating my sister's ex-boyfriend, and if not, why start a rumor you are?" I would need to make up a reason for being there, and fast.

Cheryl hung up the phone and turned to me. "So, what brings you here?"

"I'm, uh, planning a book release party in a few months when I finish my current novel and I'm looking for volunteers to help organize it." I settled back, releasing a deep breath. That should be believable.

"And you heard how wonderful I am at parties?" Cheryl clapped her hands together. "I'd love to spearhead the release party. You should be finished with your book soon, right? After all, you shouldn't keep your fans waiting too long."

I'd heard that before. I got Cheryl's phone number and told her I'd be with her as soon as I knew a release date. It never failed to amaze me how ignorant people actually were about the publishing process. It would take at least a year for me to write the book, have it go through the editing process, and then actually be released to stores. Still, I felt as if I'd covered my tracks nicely in coming up with an excuse to visit the station.

After peering around the corner to make sure Angela was nowhere in sight, I rushed to my car and drove to the bank to cosign a loan for Mom. I arrived five minutes early, surprised to see Mom already seated in the manager's office.

"Yoo-hoo!" She waved through the glass window, attracting the attention of everyone in the bank.

I sighed and made my way to her side. "Hey, Mom."

"Sweetie, this is Robert Smithfield. He's the new banker."

"Pleased to meet a famous author." He held out

his hand, surprising me by his grip. Somehow, I tended to view bankers, especially ones who were only a couple of inches taller than me and soft around the middle, to have weak handshakes. "I'm a fan."

"Thank you." Wow. I'd met two new fans in one day. Being a local celebrity wasn't something I thought I would enjoy. It was much safer in my own little community where the neighbors thought I wrote smut and avoided me at all costs.

"If you're cosigning this loan, Miss Nelson," Mr. Smithfield said, "I see no reason why we can't proceed. Fifty thousand dollars is quite a lot of money, but with your house as collateral, it is very doable."

My heart stopped. Fifty thousand dollars? Was Mom crazy? "Uh, do we really need that much?"

"Well, if we don't use it, we can just give it back." Mom looked at me as if I was dense. "I need a lot of things and will have to hire help. I thought you were going to do this with me."

"I am." I just hadn't thought of putting my house up as collateral. What if my stalker killed me? What would happen to my beautiful Victorian then? "Fine. Let's do this." My stomach churned. I wiped sweaty palms on the thighs of my denim Capris. What had happened to my peaceful, orderly life?

Once I'd signed my life away, praying Mom would do a good enough business to pay off the loan herself, I walked with her to her car. "I need you to come with me to order the store sign," she said.

"I have to get home and write. I have a stalker waiting for the next book, remember?"

"Oh, pooh." Mom waved a hand. "Tell that moron it takes a while to write a book and that you have a life."

"I might not have one if I get killed." Good grief, I was now spouting her type of logic. I spotted Mr. Smithfield watching from the bank window.

"Okay, but you know how easily I get talked into things."

I must get it from her. "I'll see you at home. There's a casserole thawing on the counter." Because of my tendency to cook casseroles when stressed, I always had a supply in the freezer for busy days. I hurried to my car before she could ask something else of me.

Behind the wheel of the Prius, I glanced up to see Mr. Smithfield still watching through the bank window. He raised a hand in a wave and turned. Strange behavior, but maybe he made a habit of staring outside to observe the weather. But, he *had* seemed overly interested in me and Mom.

My cell phone rang as I pulled into my garage. I glanced at the caller id and cringed. "Hey, Angela."

"Did you confront Wayne about breaking up with me?" Her screeching threatened to burst my eardrums and reach heaven.

"No, not exactly."

"Define not exactly."

"I just wanted to see whether he really was dating Cheryl. He said he wasn't and couldn't stand the woman."

"Oh, okay, then. I gotta go. Wayne said to mind your own business." Click.

Well, at least they were talking to each other. Grabbing my purse, I slid from the car and made my way to my office. The email I'd received the other day still sat in the printer. Yesterday, being Sunday, I hadn't received one. My stalker must take the Sabbath off from harassing me.

I sat and stared at my screen, afraid to turn on my laptop. The phone rang, startling me. I grabbed my cell. "Hello?"

"It's your agent, Elizabeth, in case you've forgotten."

I wracked my brain trying to remember what I had actually forgotten. "I got nothing."

"Who is Cheryl Isaacson and why is she sending me emails about a book release party?"

I sighed. "She's a fan. I'm so sorry. I had no idea she would be contacting you."

"She's wanting me to negotiate fifty free books to go to her so she can promote you. Is she insane?"

"Maybe a little." I leaned back in my chair. "What did you say to her?"

"I didn't make her happy, that's for sure, and I told her the book wasn't scheduled for release until this time next year. She asked me to put a rush on it. It isn't written yet, is it?"

I closed my eyes. "No."

"Oh, and one more thing." Elizabeth took a deep breath. "Why am I getting emails from an unknown source threatening me if you don't finish this book quickly?"

"What?" I straightened. "You're getting them too?" Matt was going to blow a gasket.

"Have you been getting them?"

"It's just a crazy fan. Nothing to worry about, I'm sure." I turned on my laptop. "I have the police investigating. They haven't found anything to concern me yet."

"Be careful, Stormi. You can't take these things lightly."

"You be careful, too. I'll keep you posted. Bye."

We hung up and I clicked the tab for my emails.

I had two from my mysterious non-friend. Rather than opening them, I dialed Matt's number. After explaining to him about the new emails and my agent receiving one, I headed to the kitchen to fix sandwiches. He was always easier to talk with about things like stalkers and killers on a full stomach.

The doorbell rang ten minutes later. I took a deep breath and let Matt in. "Are you hungry?" I handed him a plate with a ham and grilled cheese and baked potato chips.

"Stormi, what am I going to do with you?" He took the plate.

I shrugged.

"After I take a look at the emails, we need to talk about you harassing Wayne at work on behalf of your sister."

Good grief.

7

After a thorough lecture from Matt, then some rather steamy kisses that left me confident in our relationship and a bit dizzy, I slid a casserole of spaghetti noodles, spicy sauce and cheese into the oven to heat through. While that warmed, I grabbed a tall glass of iced diet cola, called to Sadie to join me, and headed out for some alone time on the back porch.

I stared toward the hedge separating me from my new neighbors to my left. All houses were occupied now in Oak Meadow Estates except for Ms Henley's. Unless Rusty, her son, decided to return, the house could very well sit empty for as long as Ms. Henley had to remain in jail, which could very well be for the rest of her life.

The buzzing of a saw assaulted my ears. Sadie bolted toward the sound, barking with everything in her. I sighed and unfolded myself from the lawn chair I'd just sat on before following her.

"Stop it, you silly thing." I grabbed her collar and pulled her back. The sawing stopped.

"Hey!"

I glanced up to see a set of dark eyes peering over the hedge to my left. "Hey, yourself."

"I'm Tony Salazar, your new neighbor. My wife's name is Becky. You must be the author we've been warned about."

"That would be me." I glanced toward my drink and chair, not wanting to be rude, but craving a few moments to myself before my family barged in.

"Is it true the vacant house across the road belonged to a murderer?"

"It's true."

"I read your book. It was good, but geared more toward women, don't you think?"

"They are my target audience, but thank you."

"Well, it was nice meeting you. We'll have to do it face-to-face someday." He laughed.

"Yes, we will." I started to turn, then stopped. "You wouldn't be interested in joining the Neighborhood Watch program, would you? I'm the leader and could really use some help."

"Sure. How many people have joined?"

"Just me, my mother, and you. For now." I still couldn't understand why the community wouldn't rally together to keep the streets safe.

"All righty then."

"I'm holding another meeting ... tonight. My house at seven. See you there." I shook my head at desperation to find help and headed for my drink. Sadie pulled from my grasp and bounded toward the porch as Dakota stepped outside. Sadie's tail sideswiped my glass, knocking it to the ground and spilling my soda. I sighed and picked up the glass.

While my dog and nephew raced around the

yard like a couple of mad animals, I headed inside to check on dinner. Angela sat at the table, a stack of mail in front of her. "I don't understand why it's taking so long," she said.

"What?"

"I sent in a submission to sell beauty products. You know, kind of like Mary Kay or Avon? Except better. Much better."

"Do you have time while working at the station?" I opened the oven and peered inside. The cheese was brown and toasty. I turned off the oven and set the casserole on top of the stove before sliding in a pan of garlic bread. One thing or another had kept me from obtaining the word count I'd wanted to reach on my manuscript.

"I need to make more money so I can get a place of my own for me and the kids."

"I have plenty of room, Angela." While I still had moments where I craved solitude, I realized how lonely living alone had been.

"I know, but I hate living off your charity." Her shoulders slumped. "Plus, I can't bring a man back here."

"I thought you chose a more … chaste lifestyle after having your kids." Eew. I shuddered just thinking about my sister doing the sheet tango in my house.

"I did. I'm not talking about that." She glared. "What if I just want to hang out and watch a movie? Mom will pop in every two seconds asking if we want something. Don't forget how she was when we were teenagers. I doubt she's changed much."

"True." I bit the inside of my lip. "What if we fix up the basement into a private apartment for you? The kids could still sleep where they are and you can pay rent." I grinned. "That ought to help you feel more self-sufficient." And help me re-coop some of the cost of the renovations.

"I'd rather the apartment be fixed up for me." Mom marched into the kitchen.

"How long were you standing there?" Angela clasped a hand to her chest.

"Long enough to know you're up to no good." She tossed her purse on the counter and reached into the cabinet for plates. "I would enjoy having my own place, especially now that I'm a business owner. This place has a tendency to get noisy."

Seriously? That was my main complaint, but writing with a house full of people was doable when the teenagers were always gone and the adults working.

"Plus, I have a date on Friday night. What if it becomes something more and I want a little privacy of my own? And before your minds go to the gutter, remember I'm a Godly woman." She gave us both the 'Mom Look' before setting a plate at each seat.

"Well, if Mom wants the basement, I get the top floor." Angela gave a decisive nod.

"I'm not giving up my master bedroom." Was she nuts? "If you want an entire floor, then clean the attic. It's got a small bathroom, a bedroom, and a sitting area. All it needs is a little updating."

"Then I get Mom's room." Cherokee plopped into her seat. "It's bigger than the one I'm in."

"For heaven's sake." Mom set the casserole on pot holders in the center of the table. "You girls sure know how to make a ruckus."

"Wait a minute." In all the bedroom moving and house renovation comments, I'd almost skipped over one very important bit of news. "You have a date?"

"Why do you look so shocked?" She thrust open the back door. "Dakota, it's time to eat!"

"Well, it's … you haven't seemed to have much interest in the last few years." I set out eating utensils and slid the slices of bread into a bowl.

"Maybe I didn't feel it was the right time."

"Who's your date, Grandma?" Cherokee asked.

"Robert Smithfield. He's a banker."

I frowned. If I had a suspect list, which I didn't yet, he would be on it. No trustworthy man stared through a window at two women, unless … oh, he'd been looking at Mom. Fine, I'd scratch him from my soon-to-be suspect list. "Be careful. We need to eat and get things cleaned up. I'm having a meeting of the Neighborhood Watch tonight. The new neighbors actually joined." I smiled at Mom. "That means, you and I only have to patrol every other night."

"I don't mind. It gives me my exercise."

I agreed. I'd still head out each evening to walk Sadie, but it was nice knowing I didn't have to if I felt like taking a night off.

We gathered around the table, I said the blessing, and we dug in. I loved the simple dish of baked spaghetti with slices of chicken smothered in cheese. Paired with homemade garlic bread, it was one of my favorite meals.

After eating, everyone scattered, leaving the cleanup to me and Mom, as usual. "Are you sure you don't mind going to the basement?" I asked.

"Absolutely not. I'll love having my independence, and I can experiment with new recipes without hogging your stove. I'll still have my suppers with all of you, unless I have a guest." She winked.

I wanted to be happy for her. I really did, but I

still had a nagging feeling at the back of my mind that Mr. Smithfield wasn't all that he seemed. After the last run-in with a killer, I tended to be more cautious where my family was concerned.

The doorbell rang. I glanced at the clock. Our new neighbors were fifteen minutes early. "I'll get the door. Can you whip up some kind of dessert?" I asked Mom.

"You bet."

I hurried to let the newest watch members into the house surprised to discover they were both 'little people'. Mark had to have been standing on something when I spoke to him over the fence. I offered my hand to shake. "I'm Stormi Nelson, please come in."

Tony introduced his wife, a woman so cute I wanted to pick her up and hug her like a doll. Curly black hair, dancing eyes, I could tell we were going to be friends.

"Sorry if the saw bothered you earlier," Tony said, following me to the living room. "We're modifying the house to fit our stature."

"No problem at all." I motioned for them to sit on the sofa. "I apologize for my dog." Speaking of whom dashed into the room and immediately slathered the faces at her tongue level. "Sadie, down!" My face heated.

Becky giggled. "It's all right. I love dogs and this one is a beauty. Irish Wolfhound, right?"

"That's what I've been told."

Becky peeled back Sadie's lips. "She's about a year old. Beautiful." At my questioning look, she added, "I'm a veterinarian."

"It could come in handy having you next door. This big goof gets into all kinds of trouble." I snapped my fingers and motioned Sadie to sit at my feet. She did, but kept her big eyes on the newcomers. Silly dog. If I were to get conked on the head as my predecessor did, Sadie would be more than happy to join the little people family. They could ride her whenever they needed to go somewhere.

"So." Tony rubbed his hands together. "What do we do in this watch program?"

"Mom and I have been patrolling the two streets that comprise Oak Meadow Estates ourselves every night, but if we can switch off, that would be wonderful." I shook my head to indicate to my surprised mother not to say anything that would embarrass me in front of our guests. I knew how she could blurt out something without thinking first.

"I'm Anne Nelson." Mom set a tray of petit fours on the coffee table. "I made these the right size, it appears."

I palmed my head and closed my eyes. There was no hope for her.

"These are perfect," Becky giggled. "And you are hysterical."

"Why, thank you." Mom sat in a winged chair that matched the one I sat on. "Aren't you afraid to patrol the streets at your size?"

Tony's smile faded. "I carry pepper spray. I'm actually quite strong, Mrs. Nelson. Don't let my size fool you."

"I don't mean any disrespect, but I wouldn't want to go out at night alone and I'm twice as tall as you."

"You're also twenty years older," he replied, reaching for a dessert.

"Touché." Mom laughed. "I like you. I can tell

right off about a person. It's a gift. We're going to get along just fine."

"All we do is walk the streets and take a close look at everything. If you see anything suspicious, then alert the police. Also, the neighbors may alert you to concerns of their own. If they do, just make a note of them and let me know. It's that simple. I usually carry a clipboard with me, but you don't have to." I gave Mom a stern look to tell her to keep her mouth shut about my finding a dead body on my first night.

What were the chances history would repeat itself?

8

The Salazars had wanted to do patrol their first night and left a note on my front door the next morning that all was quiet. I smiled, putting on my walking shoes. Come summer, they'd change their tune quick enough when every lawn had a neighbor putting around in it.

Speaking of lawns. Mine had suffered terribly since Rusty left shortly before his mother's arrest. I needed to think seriously about hiring a landscaper before neighbors complained. "Let's go for a walk, Sadie." I clicked the leash on her collar and waited for Mom to join me.

She didn't always accompany me on patrol, but since the fiasco a few months ago, and Matt's and Koontz's warnings about not going anywhere alone, she tried to come with me at every possible opportunity, and she always dressed in black, just in case we needed to hide. Tonight was no exception.

Mom skipped up to me in black sweats, a black beanie pulled low over her hair. "I'm ready." She shook her head at my bubblegum pink sweat pants and gray sweatshirt. "You'll never blend in, will you?" She headed past me and out the door.

Sighing, I followed. "The chances of us stumbling across another dead body are slim."

"True, but if your stalker is watching," Her gaze swept over me. "You stick out like cotton candy."

I stepped off the porch and marched down the sidewalk, tossing a wave toward the Salazars. I wondered if they knew about the Edgarses and how many bullets had punctured their wall. It wasn't up to me to divulge that information. Nor was it up to me to let them know the prior tenants had been in the Witness Protection Program and had to move because they got involved with me. They seemed like nice people, why scare them off?

"Good evening!" Mom called to Mrs. Olson, who stopped her husband from pulling weeds and ushered him into the house.

"Why do you tease her like that?" I asked. "You know how she is about her husband." I still couldn't understand why the woman thought everyone was after him, but love is blind, or so they say.

"That's what makes it so much fun." She pulled a small penlight out of her beanie and shined it in the bushes.

"Sadie will bark if anyone is sneaking around."

"That dog barks when she shouldn't and hides when she should bark. I can't rely on her for protection."

"Hush, she'll hear you." I covered Sadie's ears. "This girl would take a bullet for me if the need arose." Sure, she was a big scaredy-cat, but if it came down to danger aimed at me, she'd do the right thing. I hoped.

I shivered against the chilly autumn breeze and

increased my pace. Mom could peer under every rock and twig if she wanted to, but this girl wanted to get home where it was warm. I needed to see if I had any more disturbing emails. Checking for them had become almost obsessive.

We turned the corner. I froze. Ahead, dressed in a trench coat and spy hat was the same figure I'd seen while cleaning Mom's store. I couldn't make out any distinguishing facial features in the dark, but I had little doubt now that this person wasn't following me.

"What is it?" Mom shined her flashlight in that direction. The person darted away.

"I think my stalker is following us."

"Really?" She spun, her light illuminating house windows and lamp posts. Porch lights flickered on as she disturbed folks settling down in their evening routines.

I grabbed her elbow and tugged her after me. "Turn that off before we get yelled at."

"Don't we want people to look out? What if your stalker turns violent?"

"I have my pepper spray."

"Darn it, I forgot mine." Mom glanced around us. "Every time I go somewhere with you my life is in danger."

I rolled my eyes. "Let's finish this walk and get home."

"Let's go grab an ice cream."

"It's cold out."

Mom shrugged. "I feel like a hot fudge sundae."

"Fine." We continued down the street and out of the development, reaching the ice cream parlor fifteen minutes before they closed. While I didn't understand ice cream on a cold night at almost nine o'clock, I couldn't turn it down once we were inside, leaving Sadie tied to a lamp post outside the door. I ordered yogurt with granola on top and chose a table near the window.

While I waited for Mom to add her five pounds of toppings to her sundae, I glanced out the window. I never tired of gazing on Main Street no matter the season. During spring the place abounded with flowers, summer brought painted window fronts and colorful flags, autumn brought fall foliage with gourds and pumpkins, while winter brought an abundant of Christmas decorations to be enjoyed through February. Tonight, though, all I could see was the coated person staring at me from across the street.

I bolted from my seat and out the front door. "Hey!" My sneakered feet slapped the sidewalk as I sprinted after the stalker. "Stop and face me you coward." I plunged my hand into my pocket and pulled out my pepper spray. If I caught up with the stranger, they'd regret ever following me around.

We raced down an alley. At the end, a street lamp had burned out, casting the area into a variety of shadows. My stalker stopped at the end and turned to face me. Without being able to see their face, the person reminded me of one of those faceless mask costumes that teenagers favored at Halloween. I stopped about fifty feet from them. There was absolutely no way in Hades I was taking one step closer.

It all came down to a standoff until Sadie came to my side, barking her fool head off. The stranger jumped on top of some boxes and then scaled over a chain link fence, struggling a bit to get over.

"I sent the dog to rescue you." Mom bustled up clutching her ice cream in one hand and mine in the other. "I had to bring these because they're closing and the teenager behind the counter was giving me dirty looks."

"Sadie effectively scared away the stalker. Thanks." I took my yogurt.

"You don't sound happy."

"I was trying to discover their identity." I tossed the yogurt into a nearby dumpster. "This is the second time I've seen him. I spotted them on Saturday when I went for coffee."

"You need to let Matt know," she mumbled around a mouthful of fudge.

"I will." As soon as I checked my emails to see whether I had more to tell him. I never should have decided to switch genres. Sweet, slightly heated, romances weren't dangerous in the least. But no, my agent wanted me to get out more. All that accomplished was me stumbling over a dead body and almost getting myself killed, not to mention this newest danger. Still, I was now hooked on using real life mysteries as plots for my books. I couldn't see a way out.

Thirty minutes later, we arrived home to discover Matt waiting on the front porch swing. I grinned, released Sadie from her leash, and rushed to greet him with a big kiss. I slid up under his arms, pressing close for warmth and security.

"What's wrong?" Matt tipped my face to his.

"I have a stalker."

"I know that."

"No, I mean, I have someone who follows me and dresses in a trench coat and hat. Mom and I just saw him on our walk." I laid my cheek against his chest. "I can't tell whether they are male or female."

He pulled me into the house. "How long has this been going on?"

"I first spotted him on Saturday, but wasn't sure they were following me. Now, I'm sure. Mom and I saw him twice tonight. Sadie scared them off."

He frowned. "Let's go make some coffee. I'm calling Koontz. We have some things to figure out."

I nodded and headed for the coffee pot while he pressed buttons on his cell phone. Mom soon joined us and set out four cups. She was no longer dressed all in black, having changed her top to a forest green, long-sleeved tee shirt, of which I was grateful. Her spy clothes only served as a reminder that danger crept closer. Soon, the heady aroma of percolating coffee filled the kitchen.

While Matt conversed on his phone, I headed to my office to unplug my laptop and carry it back to the kitchen. If I was going to have an audience while I checked my emails, I might as well give us plenty of room to gather around the screen.

The doorbell rang, setting Sadie barking, and Mom hurried to answer it. Koontz entered, filling the kitchen with his bulk. "So, what's happening?" He swung a kitchen chair around and straddled it.

"Stormi's stalker is now showing themselves in physical form," Matt said. "She spotted the person on Saturday and twice tonight."

"You make it sound as if we're dealing with something alien." Appeared in physical form. That struck me as funny, and I concentrated on pouring the coffee in order not to get caught grinning and lectured because danger wasn't funny.

"The culprit is escalating in their behavior," Koontz said. "I make it a habit to frequent the coffee shop as often as possible, and there are a lot of regulars. I'm trying to chat each of them up in order to get a name to do a search on, but some of them get pretty upset about being disturbed. Seems like there are an awful lot of wannabe authors that hang out there."

"Free wifi," I said, handing each of the men a cup of coffee before pouring some for Mom and I. "Plus, there's a certain stigma to writing while surrounded by books and readers."

I set my coffee next to my laptop, then sat in my chair and waited until the guys decided it was time to check the emails. They stared at each other over the rim of their cups. By this time, I knew Matt well enough to know he was trying to figure out more ways of keeping me confined to my house. Need I remind him I was abducted from my home six months ago? If someone wants me, there are ways of getting close. I cared more about the safety of my family.

"I need you to help me keep a closer eye on Stormi," Matt said, setting his cup with precision on the table in front of him. "I know she won't stay in the house, even though she's recently installed a security system. I try to be around as much as possible, but with work … maybe the two of us could take turns?"

Ooops. I keep forgetting to set the alarm, a bit of information I decided to keep to myself.

"We have an alarm?" Mom stared wide-eyed around the table.

Maybe it was a good thing she would soon have her own apartment in the basement. "I keep forgetting to set it." I avoided Matt's gaze and turned on my laptop.

He sighed heavily. "She's a lost cause, Ryan.

Sometimes I think I'd rather be tackled by you then have to talk sense into her."

Koontz laughed. "College sure was fun." He speared me with a dark-eyed gaze. "Look, girl. We're trying to do our part to keep you breathing, but you gotta help us here. That means setting your alarm, not going anywhere alone, listening to your man—"

"I listen."

"Not very well," Matt added.

The hurt in his voice brought tears to my eyes. "I'm sorry. I'll do better, I promise. But I can't sit around and let my family be in danger. You need my help finding out who is threatening me."

"Then do your research from the safety of your house," he said. "With the alarm set."

I nodded and pulled up my email. "I've got a message from my friend."

Matt and Koontz stood and moved to each side of me. I opened the email and read.

"How is it possible for you to be writing while wandering the streets and having ice cream? It seems as if you have too many distractions in your life. I will have to help you cut down on them."

9

"What do they mean?" I glanced into Matt's worried eyes. Cut down on my distractions? That could only mean my family ... or Matt. Suddenly, writing my novels had lost some of its joy. Instead of working at something I loved, I had to work in order to prevent something horrible from happening.

I leaped from my chair. "I need to get busy on my book."

Matt put a hand on my shoulder and eased me back down. "No, you'll sit here until we decide what to do." He and Koontz resumed their seats.

"Mom, do you still have the keys to Dad's old hunting cabin?" I could stay there while I wrote my book. No distractions, no worries over danger to my family. My mind leaped from one possibility to the next. If we no longer owned Dad's cabin, I'd rent one.

"Yes---"

"Absolutely not." Matt glowered. "You will not head off somewhere remote on your own."

"I don't know what else to do!" Tears stung my

eyes. If I didn't get away, I might lose someone very close to me. "This ... this freak, is watching every move I make. They're probably listening to us right now."

Matt froze, then motioned his head for Koontz to head to the other room. Koontz nodded and carefully slid back his chair and soft-stepped away from us. Matt held a finger to his lips. Oh, no. I might have landed on something. I might really have an uninvited guest. Would the perpetrator be upset that I'd called them a freak? I folded my arms and rested my head on the tabletop.

Mom patted my shoulder. "I suppose we could all take a little vacation."

"No. I won't endanger you. Either I go or you go, but we won't stay together."

"Hogwash." Mom slapped the table top. "We're family."

Matt put his lips against my ear. His breath sent my nerves tingling. "Stop talking," he whispered before straightening.

I nodded. I didn't want any potential eavesdroppers to know what I was considering. Of course, the wacko after me would more than likely be pleased. With my family gone, I could focus on writing this story they insisted I create. A story where they took center stage.

I pulled up my file and started to type, describing the crazed maniac killer as a poor unfortunate soul who lived alone, so severely disfigured that children ran screaming into the night at a mere glimpse of them. If my stalker wanted a story of their own, they would get one no one would soon forget.

"What are you doing?" Mom's horrified gasp filled the kitchen as she read over my shoulder.

"Writing."

She clamped her lips closed and stomped to the other side of the room as Koontz reentered the kitchen, a small silver disc in the palm of his large hand. "Termites."

"Good grief," Mom said. "I'll call the exterminator in the morning."

I glanced up from my screen. Seriously? Seconds later the growl of the garbage disposer sounded as it ate our little bug. "Are there more?"

Koontz shrugged. "I'll have a team check it out in the morning. Please, use the alarm."

Angela waltzed into the room, took one look at Koontz, and simpered, batting her eyes. I shook my head, wanting to tell the big man to run as far and as fast as he could to escape her clutches, but then decided he was big enough to handle my sister.

"What's going on?" Angela glanced from one of us to the other.

"We have bugs." Mom sighed. "As if we don't have enough to deal with. It's these old houses. There's always something to be done."

I feared the stress of back-to-back murder mysteries was affecting Mom's mind. I typed that we were bugged on my laptop screen, showed it to Angela, then erased the words. She nodded and poured herself a cup of coffee. She blew into the hot drink while watching Mom stare out the window.

Without having taken a sip, she set her cup on the table and exhaled heavily. "I think I'm going to take the kids away for a couple of weeks. I'll plead a family emergency. Matt, you'll back me up at the station, right?"

He nodded. "Ann?"

Mom shook her head. "Not leaving. No one is."

I seriously doubted everything would be wrapped up within two weeks, and I didn't fault Mom for wanting to stay. After all, she was in the middle of opening her dream business. "Don't go, Angela. I just need to write this book as fast as humanly possible and get it off to my editor. Then my crazy stalker will leave us all alone." I hoped. I prayed.

A ding sounded, signaling a new email. Immediately everyone gathered around my laptop.

"You jumping yet?" I read.

"What the heck does that mean?" Angela asked. "You know ..." she tapped the screen with one long cotton-candy pink fingernail. "I think this person is just playing games with you to give you fodder for a new book. That's what you get when you write about things that really happen to you. People get weird and want their own minutes of fame."

Although I agreed with her as to my stalker's reasoning, I didn't appreciate her somehow making it sound as if our current fix was my fault. "I didn't plan this."

She shrugged. "Maybe not, but you sure know how to mess up things." She grabbed her coffee, tossed Koontz a dazzling smile, and sashayed out of the kitchen, informing us on her way that maybe she wouldn't leave after all. Why give some nutcase the satisfaction of running her out of her home?

Again, I agreed, but my heart still raced in overdrive at the threat to my family. I met Matt's gaze again and blinked away the tears. He pulled me out of my chair and into his arms. Never in a million years would I have thought a writer's life could be so turbulent.

"Show me again how to set the alarm, please." I'd become a hermit, only leaving my house when armed with a gun, Tazer, and accompanied by a crowd.

After planting a tender kiss on each of my eyelids, Matt led me to the front door where he once again showed me the sequence of button pushes that would help safeguard my house. "We'll have a team in here tomorrow to check for any bugs. Possibly cameras, too. Maybe you should spend the night at a hotel?"

I shook my head. "If someone has hidden cameras in my home, they've already seen everything I have to hide." I shuddered. Perverts. What could someone possibly hope to gain by spying on me? That wouldn't force me to write faster. Instead, I felt mud gathering in my brain, drowning the creative process.

Wrapping my arms around Matt's waist, I rested my forehead against his chest. "Sadie can act as a second warning system. She'd probably hide under the table, but she will at least bark first."

"I'm sorry about all this, sweetheart." His arms tightened around me. "I'm doing my best to make it go away."

I vowed right then and there to put an end to the madness as soon as possible. I couldn't chance anything happening to my family or Matt. Peering over his shoulder, I spotted Koontz speaking with Mom in a low voice. He put one beefy hand on her shoulder and steered her to the kitchen table. Her red-rimmed eyes increased the tears in mine. We were a family of strong women, but everyone has their breaking point, and I feared Mom was reaching hers.

Koontz settled her into a chair and handed her a fresh cup of coffee. He cast a stern glance our way. "I'll set up a schedule to have these folks watched at all times."

Mom patted his hand. "You're such a dear. I'm fine. Go do what you need to."

The front door slammed, sending us all racing toward the front room in time to see Cherokee and Dakota latching the bolt as the alarm squealed a warning. They clamped their hands over their ears.

"What did Aunt Stormi do now?" Cherokee yelled, rolling her eyes.

"Where have you been?" Angela stood at the top of the stairs, one hand propped on her hip. "Do you know what time it is? Do you understand the danger lurking out there?"

Matt reset the alarm. "Everything is fine. We can all relax."

"It's only ten o'clock, Mom," Dakota said. "We made curfew."

"Curfew is dusk until this … this … whatever this person is can be put behind bars." She whirled and stomped back to her room, leaving the teenagers with open mouths and scowls.

"This is all so unfair." Cherokee stormed after her mom.

Fresh tears sprang to my eyes. Since when did I become so weepy? Maybe when fear and worry became such an integral part of me.

Matt cupped my face in his hands, twining his fingers in my hair and touching his forehead to mine. "I know exactly what is going through that lovely mind of yours. Stop it. We will take care of this and you can go on writing your delightful stories without harassment."

If only I could believe him. I cast my eyes toward the window covered by thick curtains. I'd let him do his part to keep me and mine safe, but I'd also

69

be doing everything I could, too. Sitting back and waiting for something to happen or for someone to dig up a vital piece of information wasn't something I could do. Not after having successfully solved one murder mystery. There might be a lunatic lurking outside my door, but I resolved to catch the person before he could do any damage.

"The wheels are turning." Matt dragged me into the kitchen. "I can't stress enough the importance of you laying low while we catch this guy."

"And I can't tell you how important it is that I do something to help." I pulled away. "If I sit and twiddle my thumbs, I'll go stark-raving mad."

"Then snoop via the internet." He ran his hands through his hair, causing the golden strands to stick up like porcupine quills.

"Okay."

He didn't say I had to use *my* internet. While I vowed to be safe, I wouldn't be a prisoner. Angela was right in that regard. We could not let this twisted email stalker dictate our lives.

"I'm also going to leak information that my next book will be released in the next month or two. This might help get this person to back off a little."

"That's a good idea."

I could see in his eyes that I'd already lost him and that, if anything, he thought my plan would keep me too busy to venture out and get into trouble. After a quick kiss on my lips, Matt joined Koontz by the front door, promising to check in on me in the morning. I waved him out, locked the door, and reset the alarm. If people kept coming and going, that little chore would get old very fast.

"Well." Mom crossed her arms. "What's our

next move?"

"Nothing." I headed to the kitchen to clean up.

"We have to do something."

"Mom, you were spacing out!" I closed my laptop. "An exterminator?"

She grinned and leaned close, lowering her voice. "I want the unsub to think they've got me rattled."

"You scared me." I collected the cups and set them in the sink. "I'm working on a plan." I planted my palms against the edge of the sink. "But I'm not including you this time. I can't risk your safety."

"Pshaw! If you don't let me work with you, I'll head out on my own. Who knows what will happen then."

I turned and glared. The glint in her eyes told me she meant every word of what she said. I sighed. "Fine. We're partners."

10

I decided to follow Matt's advice for at least part of the day. Instead of heading to Heavenly Bakes with Mom or to the coffee shop for some people watching, I decided to perch on the window seat in the under-renovation turret room and peer through binoculars at the neighbors. The glass of the round room gave me plenty of vantage points in which to snoop.

Dust billowed from the tattered cushion in front of the window, causing me to sneeze. I glanced around as if someone could hear me, then chuckled from embarrassment. No one was home and no one had ventured to that particular room since I'd bought the house. While the floor appeared to be sturdy enough to walk on, I had tread carefully and prayed I didn't fall through.

Barely eight o'clock in the morning and the street was hopping as folks headed to work or school. The Olsons, both around retirement age, raked leaves in their front yard, Mrs. Olson giving the evil eye to any woman who happened to glance her way. With the binoculars, I could spot Mrs. Carter, wearing a lime green house dress as she watered her autumn flowers. Regular, eccentric neighbors. Nothing out of the ordinary.

Now, my new neighbors to the left were a whole other story. Mark Wood loaded something rolled in an area rug into the back of a utility van while his wife, Diane, peered up and down the street. When the Salazar's stepped out to push their trash can to the side of the road, Mark and Diane grinned and moved away from the van. Very curious. What was rolled in their rug?

Tony Salazar raised up on his tiptoes to peer around Mark. Mark stepped to the side while Diane slammed the back of the van door closed. Spying on the neighbors was better than any daytime drama television show. Why hadn't I done it years ago?

They conversed a bit more, then the Salazars bustled back to their house. Mark waved his arms around, raising his voice to Diane but not enough so that I could hear, then slid behind the wheel of the van and drove off. Diane tossed him a 'not so nice' finger gesture and ran into her house, slamming the door behind her.

I lowered the binoculars to my lap. Did the two sets of neighbors know each other well? Had they met before moving to my community? Was that why Tony was so eager to join the Neighborhood Watch? More questions swam through my mind than before I had started spying.

Movement at the end of the street had me raising the glasses again. Matt was just getting into his car. His sister, Mary Ann, waved goodbye to him then closed the front door after her. She pulled a cell phone from her pocket.

A second later, mine rang. "I've got something for you," she sang.

"Do tell."

"It appears that your emails aren't coming just from the coffee shop. The one last night came from the library."

My heart skipped. "Want to pick me up?"

"You bet."

I clicked off the phone and dashed down the stairs, my feet raising little puffs of dust with each thud across the wood. If the turret wasn't on the third floor, I'd consider moving my office up there. Inspiration for mystery novels abounded.

Grabbing my purse from the foyer table, I rushed out the door as Mary Ann came to a halt in my driveway. I slid into the passenger seat of her Volkswagen Beetle. "You're the best snooper ever."

She grinned. "It helps having a brother who is the lead detective on the case. Of course, plastering my ear to the wall when he's on the phone doesn't hurt. Ryan Koontz came by the house after leaving your place last night, too." She backed onto the street. "They're really worried about you. Other than tracing the emails to public places, they have absolutely nothing to go on."

"I'll find out who is responsible." I clicked my seatbelt into place.

"Hopefully, before you're abducted again. My brother almost went crazy when that happened."

Her words, while warming me, also reinforced the severity of what was happening and increased my urgency to find the culprit. "I haven't been to the library since I've moved here. There isn't a lot of need since I can do my research on the internet."

"Or by living it." She flashed me a smile. "You'll need to come up with some kind of story. The librarian, Janet Dillow, is a middle-aged sourpuss who doesn't know how to smile. Although the library is a public building, she doesn't like loitering. She wants everyone to either be reading, actively browsing, or on the computers. She keeps her lines short and her expectations long."

"I can pretend to be looking for research books. Not everything needs to come from the computer." I reached over and placed a hand on her shoulder. "Thank you. With your help, maybe we can come up with some questions to ask Mrs. Dillow that will help us figure out whether my friend is spending much time there."

"If anyone can mellow her, you can. After all, it's authors like you that keep books in libraries."

Ten minutes later, we pulled up in front of a brick building with large glass windows. In the small courtyard rose a metal tree with a bench placed underneath it. A small plaque stated that it was donated so imaginations could soar. I put a hand to my heart at the gesture, wishing I had thought of donating something meaningful to the library. Maybe I could do a book-signing and donate the proceeds. That would be as good of a reason for visiting today as any other.

Side-by-side, shoulders back, looking every bit as if we were walking the Green Mile, Mary Ann and I marched into the library and to the front desk. A woman with a salt and pepper spiked do, horn-rimmed glasses, and bright red lipstick glared up at us for exactly two seconds. Then she smiled, revealing perfect white teeth.

Mary Ann gasped. "She smiled."

"Of course I smiled, you ignorant chit." Mrs. Dillow thrust out her hand. "We have a real author in the house. I must be your biggest fan."

There seemed to be a lot of them lately, which recently was not necessarily a good thing. I returned her handshake. "Mrs. Dillow, right?"

"Ms., but you may call me Janet or Jan. Doesn't matter as long as you call."

Mary Ann furrowed her brow and glanced at me in alarm before shrugging. "It's a mystery. It really is."

Janet shook her head. "Just because you're Matthew's sister doesn't mean I have to like you. Where is *For Whom The Bell Tolls*? You checked it out in high school."

"Seriously? How many times are you going to make me pay for it?" Mary Ann dug in her purse, coming out with checks in a bright pink folder. "This time, I want a receipt with your signature."

Once they had the problem with the way overdue library book taken care of, Janet again turned to me. "How may I help you?"

I glanced at the forming line behind me. "Maybe you should take care of them first."

"Aren't you just as sweet as the biography on the back of your novel?" She waved a hand. "They can wait or use the self-serve stations."

I needed to make my excuses quickly. The rude librarian was developing a gleam in her eyes that made me nervous. Were there any 'normal' people left in Oak Meadows? "I, uh, thought it would be nice to, uh …"

"For goodness sake." Mary Ann hit me with her elbow. "She's all bark and no bite. Spit it out before there's a riot."

"I would like to do a book signing and donate the proceeds to the library." There. Now to figure out how to question her about possible stalkers using the library computers.

"When would you like to do this?" Janet flipped a desk calendar.

"When my next book is released?"

She narrowed her eyes. "Isn't that going to take too long? We really should work off the momentum of your book's success. You've been spotted traipsing around town like you don't have a care in the world. How will you be able to finish your next book any time soon?"

"I'm further along than people know." Why should she be so concerned? Now, I had her badgering me about a book signing and the 9-1-1 operator clamoring for details about the release party. I'd dug myself a hole the size of a giant meteor crater.

She clapped her hands. "Wonderful! We'll do the signing in two weeks. That gives me more than enough time to advertise and post in the paper."

Mary Ann elbowed me again. "Don't you have something to research?"

"Oh, yes, of course." I forced a smile to my face and followed my friend to the non-fiction section. My brain raced with how I was going to have something to sell in two weeks. If all else failed, I'd use my prior release, *Anything For A Mystery*.

"I'll come help you as soon as I work this line," Janet said.

"You're crazy," Mary Ann whispered. "Why so quiet all of a sudden? It's like you didn't know what to say to her."

"She scares me." I ran my finger along books

about the paranormal. "I probably wouldn't have paid my missing book fine, either. Not if it meant I had to talk to her."

"Ugh. I've paid it three times and didn't get a receipt this time, either." She whirled and stormed to the front of the line, returning a few minutes later with a receipt waving from her hand. "Ta-da!"

"Shhh." Janet came up behind her as swiftly as the ghosts I was reading about. "Now, are you going to have spirits in your next book?"

I shook my head. "No, I'm actually wondering whether I could ask you a question more along the lines of something personal."

She tilted her head. "Maybe."

"Do you have regular customers who come in to use the internet? Someone who might seem a bit ... off? Secretive?"

"That's an odd request." She tapped a sculpted fingernail against her teeth. "Mostly teenagers use the internet, but occasionally a homeless person, or someone looking for a job who doesn't have a computer might come in. There're also a couple of wannabe authors who bring in their own laptops. Why?"

"It's for a character in my next book." How much should I risk telling her? I didn't want the fact that my stalker might be using the library or have her know I actually had a stalker. "The homeless man angle will work wonders."

The hard glint appeared in her eyes again. What was with the bi-polar librarian bit? I dug into my purse for a business card and handed it to her. "Give me a call when you're ready. Thank you so much." I grabbed Mary Ann's arm, this time being the one to drag her in my wake.

Once we reached the car, I couldn't get inside fast enough. Who knew being an author would garner such attention from such weirdoes? Maybe I should have used a pseudonym. Then this entire situation could have been avoided.

"I've never seen Ms. Dillow react so kindly to anyone before." Mary Ann inserted her key in the ignition. "She really must like your books. Not that I blame her. I've always thought I was your biggest fan, but …"

I rested my head back against the seat. "My stalker calls him, or herself, my biggest fan. Not counting you, I've met two people using the same tag line in the last week. Both women who are stranger than a six-legged fox."

11

Mary Ann laughed. "It's time to take some notes, but first...." She stopped in front of the coffee shop. "Drinks!"

"Then do you mind if we stop by and check on my mom?" My friend was right. It was time to start writing things down to see whether something popped up to make sense.

"I don't mind at all. We'll take her a coffee, too."

We shoved open our doors and got into the normal long line at the counter. Since it would take at least ten minutes for the Barista to take our orders, I glanced around the shop, not surprised to see Sarah hunched over her laptop. Her normally inky hair was dyed a Lucille Ball red. I was surprised to see the Salazars sharing a laptop, though. I didn't have any particular reason, but the gesture seemed odd to me. Their button eyes darted around the room. When Becky spotted me, she waved and then whispered something to her husband.

Oh, well. People around town were always talking about me. Strange behavior or not, I just couldn't picture my new neighbors as internet stalkers.

"Yeah?" Tyler, the Goth Barista, scowled at us.

Mary Ann sighed. "Three of the biggest frozen mocha coffees you got." She turned to speak over her shoulder. "I wonder why they keep this kid on the payroll. I've never seen him do anything but scowl."

"My aunt owns the place." Tyler's mouth quirked. "Besides, I love the smell."

"My apologies." Mary Ann grimaced.

Normally one of the nicest people you'd ever meet, her snarkiness that day put getting to the bottom of her mood a top priority.

"You're that mystery writer, right?" Tyler asked, taking Mary Ann's debit card but looking at me.

I nodded.

"My mom is complaining that it's taking you too long to write the next book."

"It's barely six months since the release of the last one." I shook my head. It was wonderful that readers looked forward so eagerly to the next installment, but writers had lives, too. Besides, I knew of a couple of authors who had years between their books. Did they have crazy people threatening them? I didn't think so. Only I could be that lucky.

"Yeah, I told her to be patient and stop bothering me. She's always on her laptop checking your website. It's driving me postal." Tyler handed back the card. "Art takes time. Next."

His comment about going postal sent trickles of alarm up and down my spine, but his referring to my work as art warmed me right back up. He seemed like a nice young man despite the facial piercings and long hair. Just goes to show the old adage about judging a book by its cover wasn't necessarily true.

"Wow." Mary Ann pushed the door open for me. "People are surprising me at every turn today.

Those who are usually grouchy are talking to you as if you're their lifelong friend."

"And other people are definitely out of sorts." I wiggled my eyebrows over my drink.

"I'm sorry." She sagged onto one of the seats beside a bistro-style table. "I feel as if I'm in a rut."

I glanced up and down the street before taking a seat across from her. If Matt or Koontz were to see me, there was no telling what kind of lecture I would get for sitting out in the open. "I'm sorry. What can I do to help?"

"Guide me on what I want to do with my life?"

"I thought you liked being a teacher."

"I do, but lately … well, I've felt stifled in my creativity." She took a sip of her drink. "We're told to teach what will help students past the myriad of state required tests. It's frustrating. Not every child learns the same."

"What do you want to do? Do you have a dream? A passion?"

"I want to work in the publishing industry." She twirled her straw in her cup. "I've loved to read since I was four. It's how I spend my free time."

I stared at her heart-shaped face, framed by a mass of golden curls, and acted on impulse. "How about you spend some of that free time as my assistant? This way, you can learn some things and maybe, eventually, become an editor or agent in the topsy-turvy industry of publishing."

She squealed. "Really? I'd love that! When can we start?"

I laughed. "You help me solve this mystery and get this book written and I consider you hired. I'll pay you one thousand dollars a month, but I must warn you

… I can be a tough taskmaster."

"You pay me one thousand for the rest of the school year, then if you're pleased with my performance, I quit teaching, and you raise my pay to two thousand a month and introduce me to your agent." She thrust her hand across the table. "Since today is Saturday, I will give you every weekend, Sundays after church, and all holiday breaks, plus whatever free hours I may have in the evenings when you need me."

"I don't think I'll need all that, especially in the beginning, but I do believe I've just hired me an assistant." I shook her hand. That should make my stalker happy. After all, I'd be able to write more if I wasn't having to deal with all the other things that go along with the writing career, and my agent wouldn't mind being introduced to someone so in love with the industry. Who knew? Maybe Mary Ann's next step would be as an assistant to a literary agent.

With more shrieks of delight, Mary Ann grabbed her cup, and we headed across the street to Heavenly Bakes. The windows sparkled from a fresh washing, the stoop was swept clean, and Mom sat at her desk staring at her computer.

"Wonderful," she said as she glanced up and accepted the sweaty cup of blended coffee. "I could use some caffeine."

"What are you working on?" I noticed her appliances had been delivered. The delicious aroma of baking cake filled the store.

"Orders." She sighed. "I'm going to have to hire help sooner than I'd thought. Not that I'm complaining, mind you, but word has gotten out and everyone from here to Little Rock wants a cake. The baking isn't the hard part. It's the decorating that takes so much of my time. Who has time to interview for a fabulous cake decorator?"

"Put an ad in the paper. You'll have plenty of applicants. Maybe you can hire a baker and you do the decorating." I pulled a notebook out of my purse. "I promised to let you be a part of solving this mystery. Mary Ann and I are getting ready to take some notes. Do you have time?"

She scooted back her chair. "That, I have time for." She rubbed her hands together and glanced at the clock. "Ten more minutes before the cakes come out. Let's get to work."

Mary Ann took the notebook. "As your newly hired assistant, I'll take the notes."

"Assistant?" Mom glanced from her to me.

"I could use the help to be able to devote more time to writing."

She shrugged. "Must be nice. Okay, so who is our top suspect?"

"Anyone with a computer and internet access," I said.

"Be reasonable." Mom shook her head. "I don't have all day."

"Well, there's the new 9-1-1 operator, Cheryl Isaacson, who was more than eager to help with a book release party—."

"Which is now my job," Mary Ann interrupted.

"I've already promised it to her in order to garner information." I gave her a stern look. "I can't undo what is already done. You can be my assistant from this point forward." Why couldn't life move smoothly in one direction?

Mary Ann wrote down her name. "You might as

well add Ms. Dillow to the list."

"The librarian?" Mom asked.

"Yeah, she was a little too nosey about the release of the next book, too." I chewed the inside of my cheek. "Put down Tyler and his aunt. Oh, and the Salazars and the Woods couple." I'd learned months ago to put down anyone who seemed suspicious when my life was at stake. The only problem was … I couldn't picture any of these people as an internet stalker. Everything was as dense as Mom's chocolate cake. I sent God a prayer for guidance. I really didn't want to accuse an innocent person.

Mary Ann tapped the pen on the desk top. "So, the only motive we have for someone bothering you is that they don't want to wait the time it takes for a book to be published. What if our suspect doesn't even live around here?"

"I've thought of that," I said. "But the fact I've seen someone following me who wears a trench coat kind of sent that theory out the window. Oh, and the fact someone had gone into my house and set up listening devices." A crew had electronically swept my home the day before and found nothing more than the one bug.

"You're right. It's someone local." She tapped the pen harder until Mom reached over and snatched it from her fingers. "Sorry."

I glanced at the list. "I guess my top four suspects would be Cheryl, Ms. Dillow, Tyler, and his mother. They seem the most eager for the next book." Which still didn't make sense. "There has to be more to it than this. Traditionally published books take months to a year to be released."

"It's all about the fame." The timer on the stove

sent Mom catapulting from her chair. She slipped pot holders over her hands and pulled out a dark chocolate cake and a red velvet cake. "Look how much attention Marion Henley got after killing off the folks who were mean to her simple-minded son? Why, you making your book all about her would be incentive enough for some people, I'd guess."

Could it really be that simple? "Then I'm changing my entire plot. It won't be about this mystery at all." I couldn't have fans coming out of the woodwork wanting every book to be about them. I was an imaginative author, I could write this from scratch.

"Well, you could always change it up a bit. I've heard several people say how nice it was to read about something that actually happened around here. Just change who the killer actually is to someone completely unrelated." Mom turned off the oven. "But, it's up to you. Considering how little time you actually spend writing, you could do pretty much whatever you want."

"I know. This whole thing has really set me back." I covered my face with my hands. Three months is all it would take to actually write the book, if I sat down and disciplined myself to write it. But, if I wanted to form the story about the current events, the story had yet to play itself out. "Speaking of writing, I do need to get home."

"I'll take you," Mary Ann offered. "Then I've got to head to Little Rock to pick up some teaching supplies. I'll give you a call when I return to see if you have work for me."

"You've done enough for today." I smiled. "We'll get together after church tomorrow if I come up with something."

"I'm also good with marketing and Photoshop."

She grabbed her purse off the table. "I'll work on some kind of campaign for you."

I might have to raise her salary if she did all she said she could do. "Good luck with your advertisement, Mom."

"Right." She sat back in front of her computer. "I'll do that right now."

Mary Ann dropped me off in front of my house where a stern Matt greeted me on the porch. "Good luck," Mary Ann said, tossing her brother a wave. She backed out of the drive, leaving me to face the music alone.

"At least you aren't running around town without company," Matt said. "But you did forget to set the alarm when you left."

My shoulders slumped. I'd never remember. One day, I'd arrive home to meet my stalker face-to-face.

12

We headed into the house where, of course, the green light on the alarm blinked a welcome. I sighed and dropped my purse on the foyer table, before bending to pet Sadie. "You'll keep the bad guys out, right?" Not likely. Maybe obedience training would help her be braver.

"Koontz said you went to the library." Matt followed me into the kitchen and sat at the table.

"Was he following me?"

"Him, me, one of the other officers. You won't leave the house without a tale."

I made a face. "Are you hungry? There is some leftover spaghetti."

"That sounds good." He glanced at his watch. "I have thirty minutes of lunch left. Did you find out anything?"

"Not really." I pulled the casserole dish from the refrigerator and divided what was left between two plates. "Just that Ms. Dillow is another avid fan who can't wait for my next book. I'm getting nowhere fast. Oh, and your sister wants to change careers, so I've hired her as my literary assistant. Part time for now, permanent if she goes through with it."

His eyes widened. "Literary assistant or fellow

snoop?"

"Stop it." I microwaved the leftovers. "She's unhappy where she is. We did spend time on a suspect list today." I fetched it from my purse and handed it to him. "You can copy this, but don't take it."

He shook his head. "You just can't leave it alone, can you?"

"Nope."

"Guess I'll have to deal with it, then, since I have no intentions of letting you go." He flashed a dimpled, heart-stopping grin before glancing at the list. "None of this makes sense."

"I know. We need to set a trap for the trench coat person."

"No, *we* don't. But maybe the police can." He leaned back. "Did you let the librarian know your book will be out soon?"

"Yes, and strangely enough, she didn't believe me." The microwave dinged. I retrieved our lunch and set it on the table. "I suppose it would be hard to fool her as to how long the process takes since she works with books all day."

"I guess this list is as good as any." Matt took a picture of it with his cell phone then started eating. "I don't think we're dealing with a professional, just a very smart person. Leaving bugs to eavesdrop can be learned on the internet."

I wasn't sure whether to be relieved or frightened that my stalker might be a normal everyday Joe with a psychotic problem. "Mom thinks it's someone who wants their moment of fame in my book. I'm not going to give them that. I'll use all this as the basis for the story, for lack of anything else, but the suspect will be someone of my own fabrication. I can't have this kind of stuff happening with each book in the series."

"We'll find them." He laid a hand over mine. "I'll keep you safe."

I leaned over to kiss him, knowing he'd do everything in his power to protect me, but also knowing that sometimes things were out of someone's control. "Thank you."

"You're welcome." He grinned and shoved back his chair. "I've got to get back to work. Stay home for a while, okay?" His cell phone rang. He dug it out of his pocket. "Steele here. What?"

His face lost color. His gaze latched onto mine as pain rippled across his features. "I'll be right there."

"What happened?" My heart lodged in my throat.

"Mary Ann is in the hospital. A car accident." He whirled and dashed outside.

I grabbed my purse and sprinted after him. "Wait! I'm coming, too." Without waiting for an answer, I slid into the passenger seat of his car and clicked my seatbelt into place.

Within seconds, Matt had lights flashing and a siren blaring. I often forgot his car, while looking like something a normal person would drive, was actually department issued.

We made good time to Oak Meadows General. Matt grabbed my arm and pulled me in his wake as he rushed through the Emergency room doors. Koontz greeted us at the counter. "She's unconscious. Her car veered off the road on Elbow Curve and smashed into a tree. There's her doctor." He pointed to a tall, thin man with wire-rimmed glasses and a receding hairline.

"I'm Doctor Glassen. Are you Miss Steele's next

of kin?"

Matt nodded. "Can I see her?"

He nodded. "Just keep the noise down. She hasn't woken yet. We're watching a lump on her head, and she's suffering from multiple contusions. Her prognosis is good, despite being unconscious. I'll check in with you in a few minutes."

I followed as Matt headed for her room, Koontz saying he'd head to the cafeteria and purchase three coffees. Mary Ann had to be all right. I'd driven Elbow Curve. A nasty, sharp turn with a steep dip in the road. If she'd been headed to Little Rock, why had she gone down the two-lane highway rather than the interstate?

"Does Mary Ann know anyone in that area?"

"No, why?" Matt glanced at me.

"She was headed to a teaching store. Why would she be on that road?"

He stopped outside her door. "I'm not sure, but I intend to find out." He pushed the door open and waved me through.

Mary Ann lay in a hospital bed, her face as pale as the sheets except for the scrapes and bruises that painted her skin. A monitor beeped beside her. She looked so frail under the mint green blanket spread across her, that I gasped. A goose egg rose, bluish-purple on her right temple. I gripped Matt's hand.

He squeezed back before moving to his sister's side. Reaching over, he smoothed a curl away from her face. "Hey, little Sis, open your eyes for me, okay?"

When she didn't respond, he sighed and moved to a striped chair beside the bed. "I've worried about her from the minute our parents died ten years ago."

"That's what siblings do." I put my right hand on his shoulder. "Angela is the oldest, and I think I've worried about her my entire life. Do you think her accident has anything to do with me?"

"It's possible." He rubbed his hands roughly down his face. "Somehow, your stalker seems to know every move you make, hear your conversations, know who you're—" He yanked my purse off my shoulder and dumped the contents on the bed beside Mary Ann.

"What are you looking for?"

He turned the purse inside out, ripping at a seam on the strap. He frowned and grabbed my notepad and a pen, writing, "When did you leave your purse unsupervised?"

I had to think. While I wasn't obsessive about keeping it in my sights, I still rarely left it where anyone could get to it. Wait. "At the bookstore and coffee shop. I went there to scope out possible suspects after Koontz told me the emails came from there." I sagged into the only other empty chair in the room, still writing. "I went to the restroom. Sarah Thompson said she'd watch my things, but when I returned, she was at the counter talking to someone."

He dropped a small silver disc into my hand. Gritting my teeth, I jumped up and stepped into the closet of a restroom. Seconds later, I'd flushed the offending object away and returned to Mary Ann's bedside. When was it safe to talk anymore? I slumped in my chair, watching Matt watch his sister. I could imagine the fear that ripped through him. I'd been in pretty much the same boat a few months ago when Angela and the kids had been abducted with me and led into the woods to die. God had rescued us then, and He would save Mary Ann now.

What if somehow, someone bugged my person? I wrapped my arms around my stomach. How hard would it be to slip something into my food or drink? What if I carried one of those little things in my stomach at that very moment? "I'm going to throw up."

"What?" Matt stiffened. "Why?"

"What if one of those ... things are inside me."

"You're fine, but just in case, don't eat or drink anything you didn't see prepared." He slipped his fingers under Mary Ann's hand. "She seems to be breathing okay."

"Yeah, and she's always pale, so we can't judge her color by that." I clapped a hand over my mouth as he sent me a startled glance. "Sorry. I'm pretty pale, too."

"Sometimes you say the darndest things." He chuckled. "No wonder you've stolen the hearts of both Steeles."

Had I? I hoped so, because Detective Matthew Steele was definitely in danger of stealing my heart.

Mary Ann groaned, jerking our attention back to her. Her eyes fluttered open. "Where am I? Why am I lying down?" She put a hand to her head. "Oh, my head is killing me?"

"You don't remember anything?" Matt leaned over her.

"I went to Little Rock, and ... didn't make it to the store. Something stopped me."

"A tree." I pointed out.

"No, before that." She frowned. Pushing against the mattress, she tried to sit.

"Wait." Matt handed her the button to raise her bed. "Don't move around until the doctor says so. Tell us everything you can remember."

She glanced at the items of my purse. "Why is Stormi's purse dumped all over me?"

"Let me clean that up." I put my things to rights. "Now, we're ready. Hurry before the doctor comes in and runs us out. He promised us only a few minutes."

"Oh, okay." She took a deep breath, still visibly trying to remember. "I'd driven to Little Rock and … grabbed a burger from a fast food place. I never made it to the store … and, oh, yeah! I saw the person in the trench coat, or at least someone in a trench coat. I followed them."

"To Elbow Curve." Matt groaned.

"Well, yeah, that's where the person went. If I hadn't followed him, he would have gotten away."

"Sweetie, he did get away. You had an accident." I forced a reassuring smile to my lips. Maybe the knock on the head had forced away some of her reasoning.

"I know that. I was there. I took the corner too fast."

"That's it?" Matt asked.

"That's it. Simple fact of losing control. I need to take a defensive driving course. I could add that to my resume."

"I took a self-defense class a few months ago, remember? We could take the driving class together," I offered.

"The two of you are out of your minds. We're sitting here, waiting for the doctor—"

Who chose that moment to enter the room. "Ah, my patient is awake. Wonderful. How are you feeling, Miss Steele?"

"A little sore, but good. Can I go home?"

"In the morning, if there are no repercussions to the knock on the head." He glanced at her chart. "Your visitors will have to leave."

Matt sighed and planted a kiss on Mary Ann's forehead. I moved to the other side of the bed and kissed her cheek. She grabbed our hands, and whispered, "I stomped on my brakes, but they didn't work. You might want to get a mechanic to check out what's left of my car."

13

Matt probably broke the sound barrier getting us to the mechanic. It didn't matter that the window showed a closed sign. He banged until a short, wiry man in oil-stained coveralls glared at us through the window. Matt flashed his badge.

The man muttered something from the other side of the glass and opened the door. "Make it quick. I got someplace to be."

I probably should have warned the poor guy to keep his mouth shut. Matt blasted him with enough verbal bullets the man should have been writhing on the ground in pain. Still, Roger, his name badge said, crossed his arms and took the assault like a soldier.

"Yeah, they brought the Volkswagen in a few hours ago." Roger thumbed toward the back of the building. "I ain't looked at it yet. There isn't much left."

"I want you to look at the brakes. Now. Please." Matt added the 'please' as if the word was forced through his teeth in hopes of softening the mechanic's mood. I didn't think it would work.

"Come on." Roger stomped toward huge metal doors in the back of the building. "My wife made my favorite dinner, lasagna with garlic bread, and she gets real cranky when I'm late."

"My sister is lying half-dead in the hospital. I win."

"Didn't figure it was a contest." Roger slid open the doors, giving us our first glimpse of what should have been Mary Ann's coffin.

The poor car was half of its already small size. The engine sat where Mary Ann's lap would have been.

"I heard the driver ended up in the back seat. Nasty wreck." Roger motioned toward the hole where the door used to be. "Feel free to look around."

"I'd like you to tell me whether the brakes failed and why, if possible." Matt's face had turned the shade of dry oatmeal.

My heart went out to him. I wasn't feeling so chipper myself. The sight of the mangled car would turn anyone's stomach, much less someone who cared deeply for the injured driver. Only God's mercy had Mary Ann still breathing after her encounter with that tree.

Roger muttered something that sounded a lot like a curse word under his breath, then stepped on a small plate in the floor. The plate activated a platform that rose, taking the car with it and allowing us a good view of mangled car guts.

Fifteen minutes later, Roger wiped his greasy hands on a greasier rag. "The brake lines were cut. Smooth and clean."

A muscle ticked in Matt's jaw. "You're sure?"

"Positive. Can I go home now?"

Matt nodded, gripped my elbow a bit too tightly, and dragged me to his car. Once inside, he exhaled heavily, then pounded the steering wheel. My heart lurched into my throat. Was he angry at me? Did he blame me for his sister's injuries?

He wouldn't be the only one. If I hadn't let her go with me snooping, or hired her as my assistant, she might be at home right now cooking him an overcooked supper with too sweet iced tea or too tart lemonade. I ducked my head. "I'm so sorry. This is all my fault."

"No, it isn't." He turned me to face him. "Mary Ann does what she wants, and she's been excited from the moment you moved down the street and she discovered who you are. I never could have stopped her from getting involved, short of locking her up."

"I never should have moved here." I gulped back sobs.

He turned the key in the ignition. "I'm glad you did. But right now, instead of consoling you, I have an attempted murderer to find."

His words froze me. For the first time since the meeting, I feared my nosiness might cause him to walk him away. While I couldn't blame him, especially because of the danger toward Mary Ann, I prayed he'd stay. I understood how he felt. I felt the same way in regards to my family. I'd also tried to get Mom to stop trying to help, to no avail. Unfortunately, people were going to do what they wanted despite the danger.

Regardless of the pain ripping through me, maybe it was time Matt and I took a break from each other. At least until my stalker was caught. Mary Ann wouldn't be in any shape to help me investigate, research, or any of the other things that seemed to make up my writing life. Not for a few weeks at least. That gave me some time to catch the person responsible. I straightened and took a deep breath. "Take me home."

"Stormi—" He reached out for me.

"No, you're right. I want to go home now. I've

things to figure out." I angled my body away from him and stared out the window. I swore I could hear my heart shattering.

We pulled into my driveway. I reached for the door handle, prepared to bolt. Matt grabbed the hem of my shirt. "Don't do this."

Without turning, I blinked away tears and pulled free. "It's for the best. Find my stalker. You should all be safe not hanging around me." I slammed the door and dashed into the house, leaving one of my shoes behind. No matter. Mom would bring it in when she got home.

After turning off the alarm, locking the door behind me, then resetting the alarm, I climbed the stairs two at a time. I threw myself across my bed, covered my face with my pillow, and had a good long cry.

When I'd finished, my head pounded and the clock downstairs was striking the supper hour. Maybe we could order pizza. I wasn't in the mood for much of anything, even heating up the oven. Oh, what had I done? I laid my arm across my eyes.

I'd have to relive the day when the family got home. Mom would lecture me for being a fool in sending Matt away. Most likely I was, but if I could find a way to send my family somewhere safe, I would. I'd rather be alone when evil struck.

My cell phone beeped, signaling a text. I glanced at the screen and winced. Matt informed me I couldn't get rid of him that easily as he was still the detective assigned to the case. Tossing the phone on the bed, I got up and went to the restroom to wash my face. My red-rimmed eyes came nowhere close to how Mary Ann looked. I should leave them puffy as some sort of penance.

The doorbell rang, sending Sadie rocketing from the room and down the stairs. She barked at the door, increasing the ache in my head. "Stop it." I motioned for her to sit.

I opened the door to a young man with an elaborate bouquet of lilies in his hand. "Stormi Nelson?" He asked.

"Yes."

"Sign here, please."

I took the flowers, hoping they weren't, yet wishing they were, from Matt. While my head told me sending him away was the best thing, my head had forgotten to tell my heart. I quickly signed and closed the front door before the wailing of the alarm split my skull.

Setting the vase on the kitchen table, I pulled the little card from its holder and read, "There used to be six lilies, but now one has fallen. Who will be next?"

The card fluttered to the floor. Counting my immediate family, Mary Ann, and Matt, that made six. Mary Ann had to be the one who had fallen. My stomach lurched. I headed back upstairs and pulled a suitcase from my closet. In a panic, I tossed in clothes and underwear. If I left, they'd be okay. They had to be.

No. I plopped on the bed. The only way to get this lunatic to leave me alone was to write the book. Fine. I headed to my office. I'd write all day, every day, until I passed out from exhaustion. Whatever it took. And then … I'd self-publish it to get it released as soon as possible. Once everything was said and done, I'd write a novel worthy of my publisher. Right now, my family's safety was more important. I'd write a novella. Something short and fast.

I grinned, the gesture wicked in the reflection of

my laptop screen. My stalker wouldn't know what hit them when they got a look at how I planned on portraying them. They'd be the most incompetent criminal ever known to man.

"I'm home!" Mom called up the stairs. "What's for supper?"

"Order a pizza. I'm busy."

"No need to get snippy. Why is Matt sitting in his car in front of the house? I'm going to let him in."

I leaped from my chair. "No!"

"Why not?" She glared at me from the first floor.

"I broke up with him."

"For Pete's sake." She stooped and picked up the card from the florist. She stared at it for a moment, then headed for the door. "I have no idea what this means, but I don't like it. I'm getting Matt."

I'd forgotten she didn't know about Mary Ann yet. I plopped on the top step and waited for Matt's wrath.

Within seconds he had marched into the house and climbed the stairs, taking my hands in his and pulling me to my feet. He led me into my office and closed the door. "Why didn't you call me?"

"I'm handling this on my own now."

"No, you aren't. You're having a temper tantrum out of some misplaced guilt." He shoved the card in his pocket.

I started to point out the need for fingerprints, but the hard glint in his eye told me he didn't care. "So, what do we do?" I asked. "Keep going on as we are, watching over our shoulders? Remaining as prisoners?"

"Yes, for now." He put his hands on my shoulders. "Don't send me away again, Stormi. I'm not going anywhere."

I thought about telling him about the novella I planned to write, but decided against it. The story was strictly for the purpose of sending my stalker into an angry frenzy and drawing him out into the open. Matt would only try to stop me. I'd force myself to write five thousand words a day. I'd be finished in a week and this would all be behind us.

"Why aren't you talking to me?" Pain flickered across his eyes.

"I don't know what to say. You want me to make promises we both know I won't keep."

He ran his fingers through his hair. "Then I won't ask you to make them." He turned to stare out the window. "We'll beef up security. Keeping you safe is my top priority."

Keeping him and my family safe was mine. "If you're making things safer around here, then Mary Ann should probably stay with me until this is all settled." That left me to figure out some way of keeping Matt out of harm's way. "I'll worry the entire time she's in my presence, but the police department doesn't have enough officers to watch two separate houses, do they?"

"No, they don't. It's a good idea." He flashed a sad smile. "Maybe you shouldn't be such a good writer. You tend to prompt your fans into acting … criminal."

"That's putting it mildly." I returned his smile. "Let's go tell Mom what's going on and that she'll have an officer sitting in her new store every day." She wasn't going to like it one bit, either.

"I should have stayed up north," Mom said when we told her of the day's events. "I might not have had a place to live anymore, but at least my life was peaceful. I've ordered pizza and your sister and her kids on their way here."

"I'm sorry, Mom."

She waved away my apology. "Don't worry about it. I'm just spouting off my own frustrations. I've put an ad in the paper and have two interviews lined up for tomorrow."

"Interviews?" Matt asked.

"For a baker." She grinned. "With my luck, I'll probably hire the stalker without knowing it."

That wasn't funny.

14

Mom asked me to sit in on the baking interviews, not that I baked, cooking was more my style, but there I sat, eyes gritty from staying up until the wee hours of the night writing. We were on our fourth candidate, and I despaired of finding anyone who could bake a cookie, much less a cake.

"We're getting nowhere fast." I glanced out the window to where Koontz sat across the street at the coffee shop, his favorite place to be when Mom and I were at Heavenly Bakes. I wished I was there with him.

"Mary Ann will be released from the hospital today, correct?" Mom flipped through the pages on her desk.

"Yes." I'd have her get started right away on making a book cover for my novella which I worked on in-between interviews. A sense of wickedness came over me as I had the antagonist trip and fall, scraping his face against the rocks.

"There's our last appointment." Mom stood to greet the older woman who bustled into the shop. The woman was a cliché. Round and portly, snow-white hair, and rosy cheeks, she looked exactly how any child would view Mrs. Santa.

"Gracious, the wind has a bite to it today." She

grinned, revealing perfectly straight teeth. "I'm Greta Folsom. You're new baker."

I liked her already.

"Let's see your credentials." Mom waggled her fingers. "I'm Ann Nelson, the one you need to impress."

"Oh, honey, I can do better than pictures on paper." Greta pulled a tin from a large bag over her shoulder. "I brought samples."

Mom's eyes widened and I salivated. Until we saw the samples, of course. Too thin icing and soggy frosted flowers adorned cupcakes in different flavors. "Never mind the decorating," Greta said. "That isn't what you'll hire me for. You decorate and I'll bake. I guarantee it." She set the tin on the desk and handed each of us a fork.

My first bite of a moist red velvet cake convinced me Mom had her helper. From the look on Mom's face, she knew it, too. "You're hired, right after we do a background check." Mom handed Greta a form to fill out. "Can you start as soon as the information comes back?"

"Are you busy now?"

Mom nodded.

"Then I can start now. If you find something on me, you can tell me to get lost." Greta hung her bag on a hook on the wall. "Now, show me how to check for orders."

Mom looked as if she'd won the lottery. "Tell Matthew to rush her background check through. I've hit the gold mine."

Once Greta handed me her form, I hurried across the street to Koontz. "Mom's hired help. Rush it through, okay? I don't want to leave her until I know this woman is legit."

"I'll do it now." He headed for his squad car as I sprinted back across the street, eyes darting everywhere in case my trench coat-wearing friend was around. I doubted Greta was the culprit. The person following me was thin and of average height.

When I re-entered the shop, Mom and Greta were crowded around the computer discussing the week's work and what they could bake to display in the cases. "We should also make a few things each day to sell right from the counter," Greta said. "And serve exotic teas. We might have to hire a teenager to work part time."

"I already have more work than I can handle." Mom glanced up with a glare.

"Only make one specialty item for each day. List the menu on the outside window."

Greta seemed undisturbed by Mom's dirty looks. But I knew what they meant. She was feeling as if someone was stepping on her toes.

"There's also a website where you can buy cardboard cakes, cookies, and such. All you have to do is decorate them. Then, along with professional photographs, you have a stylish display."

Mom nodded, obviously having decided to not take offense. "You've some good ideas. Just remember who the boss is."

"I won't forget." Greta went to move my laptop. "What's this?"

"A book I'm writing." The people in this town were too nosy to mention. I took my laptop from her and stepped back.

"I thought you looked familiar." She studied my face. "I'd hate to be the person you're writing about. That wasn't a very flattering description."

"It's not meant to be." I turned and slid the computer into the laptop bag hanging beside Greta's bag. I bumped hers, sending it swaying. "Sorry." I grabbed it to hold it still. Under my hand was the distinct outline of a handgun.

"Mom, get out of the store. Now!" I grabbed her arm.

"What are you doing?" She yanked free and planted her hands on her hips.

"Greta has a gun."

"Well, of course I do. It's 2014." Greta mashed her lips together and shook her head. "No smart woman walks the streets without protection. Don't worry, sweetie." She went to pat my shoulder, but I stepped back. "If I had wanted to shoot you, I would have done it the moment I walked in the door, and I wouldn't have missed. I've never been one to wait long when there is something I want to do."

My cell phone rang. A glance at the screen told me it was Koontz. "You're mom's hired help is squeaky clean. Plays the organ at a church in Riverview and teaches Sunday School. She also has a permit to carry a weapon. And, Stormi … she's an ex-cop from way back."

My heart stopped racing. I could leave Mom in good hands. "Thanks." I hung up and turned to Greta. "Looks like you're hired. Since you're here to protect my mother, I'll leave. I have things to do." Like a quick novella to finish.

At her questioning look, Mom said, "I'll fill you in, dear. Don't worry. It's never boring around here. Life with my daughter is as volatile as her name. My other daughter, now, she's an angel."

I rolled my eyes and texted Matt that I was heading home. As I stepped out the door of the shop,

Koontz met me and drove me home. "I'll wait out here until Matt arrives," he said.

"I'll be fine. I'll set the alarm and hole up in my office. The police can't keep putting work aside to babysit me."

"Good thing this town is mostly crime free." He winked. "Except around you."

"Very funny." I unlocked the front door. "You might as well come in for coffee."

"I've had enough to fuel a plane." He headed in the house before me, took a cursory glance around, and waved me in. "But, I would enjoy a glass of ice water."

I nodded and headed for the kitchen where Sadie leaned against the counter. Her gray muzzle was deep in a plate of cake. "Get down from there." Who in the world left cake on the counter where the tallest breed of dog could easily reach? I grabbed the plate of almost eaten cake and dumped what was left of the dessert in the garbage, making sure the lid was secure when I'd finished.

Sadie promptly turned her big dark eyes on me and barfed at my feet.

"Serves you right." I swallowed back a gag and reached for the roll of paper towels.

"Let me." Koontz took the towels and knelt beside the offending mess on the floor. "You look a bit green."

"Yeah, I don't do … that very well." I took slow, deep breaths to steady my stomach.

Koontz was a gentleman. Angela should really set her sights on someone like him and leave the ones with stupid reasons for not dating her alone.

Mess cleaned and hands washed, Koontz sat at the table and fixed his coffee-colored eyes on me. "The back door is unlocked."

"What?" I whirled.

Sure enough, the deadbolt was not locked and the door hung open a fraction of an inch. Thank the Good Lord, Sadie threw up. Someone was trying to poison my dog. I should have known right away that the crumbling cake wasn't my mother's handiwork. I needed to get to writing.

"I've got work to do." I sighed. "Matt has a key, so you're free to go." I locked the back door. "Wait. If the back door was unlocked, then someone forgot to set the alarm. Again."

Who had been the last to leave? I chewed the inside of my cheek. It had to be Angela or one of her children. I couldn't get too angry, since I was guilty of forgetting myself, but my dog could have died.

"I'm taking some of this cake to the lab to be analyzed." Koontz lifted the plate from the sink and scraped the last of the crumbs into a baggie. "Hopefully, the perpetrator is playing around again, but you might want to have your dog checked by a vet."

Goodness, he was right. I snatched the phone off the wall and immediately called my vet and made an appointment. They had an opening in fifteen minutes. If they would have been busy, I would have laid my suspicions aside and given the Salazars a call. I hooked Sadie's leash to her collar. "I'm ready."

I texted Matt as to what had happened. Most likely, he and Mary Ann would beat me home. I also planned on calling a family meeting that evening. The stakes were too high. Maybe a note posted to the front door would help us all remember to set the alarm and make sure all doors and windows were locked. It was worth a try.

Koontz was a dear, maybe I should start calling him Ryan, and got me to the vet in record time. The veterinarian rushed us through, then left me in a small room while they took away my baby. I sat and read every poster on the wall until I felt I'd memorized every detail.

Eons later, the vet returned, a smile in place, and put Sadie's leash in my hand. "She's fine. Just a bit ill from imbibing too many sweets. Be careful, though. She might have problems from the other end, today." Gross.

Thank you, God, that other than some internal problems, she would be okay. I planted a kiss between my furry child's eyes and hurried to pay my bill. Thank goodness, my cats, Ebony and Ivory, who stayed out of sight most of the time since I'd brought the giant dog home, weren't prone to eating people food. Add in the fact they distrusted strangers of any kind, I rest assured as to their safety. The worst thing that had happened to them because of my snooping was their getting locked in the pantry a few months ago when someone broke into the house.

Ryan dropped me off at home where Matt was helping a battered Mary Ann from his car. They conversed briefly about the latest development, then settled Mary Ann on the sofa. I'd already made up the guest room, but knew my best friend well enough to know she would want to be in the middle of the action as much as possible.

"I've put in for a leave of absence," Matt stated, plumping pillows behind his sister. "I need to be around more and out scouring the evidence without the department breathing down my neck."

"Did you use your sister as an excuse?" Ryan

asked.

"Yep." Matt speared him a glance. "I need you to back me up, partner."

"Man, I've got your back. I'd take off and sit shotgun with you if I thought it would help."

My eyes burned at the strength of their friendship, knowing that either man would take a bullet for me or my family. Still, I knew that having Matt around twenty-four seven would put a serious damper on my own investigating. But, being the resourceful woman I was, I'd come up with ways of ditching him.

Later that evening, my entire family, plus Matt and Mary Ann gathered around the kitchen table. Everyone sat except for Matt who paced like a caged jungle cat. While I admired the view, very much in fact, his pacing set my nerves on edge. It wasn't hard to figure out that he was trying to come up with a diplomatic way of telling us we needed to follow the rules if we wanted to stay alive.

"This is the way it has to happen." He spread his legs shoulder-width apart, crossed his arms, and scanned the table with a steely-eyed gaze. "The alarm must be set when you leave and when you arrive home. No one goes anywhere alone. If I could lock all of you in this house, I would." He raised a hand against the protests of the two teenagers.

"I realize that is unreasonable. I will be sleeping on the sofa during the nights and spending most of my days prowling the streets for Stormi's stalker. Nothing I haven't already been doing, but by taking a leave from work, I can focus solely on this case and not be stretched." His gaze met mine. "This needs to come to a close, and I intend to make sure it does."

Him and I both. A few more days and my

novella would be finished, and it was a doozy!

15

Again, I'd stayed up too late writing. I leaned against the wall in the shower and lifted my face to the spray. Tired and wanting nothing more than to crawl back in bed, I was happy with my writing progress. I'd called my agent before falling asleep and left a message on her answering machine in regards to the novella being released between novels. She wouldn't mind. Anything that increased book sales, and there was no doubt in my mind that this gritty little story wouldn't send sales sky-rocketing. Especially once readers found out why I'd written it.

Oh, how I missed the simple days before my agent told me to get out more. That little activity had brought me nothing but trouble.

I turned off the shower and went to check on Mary Ann. She still slept, most likely because of her pain meds. I softly closed her door and headed to the kitchen for coffee and a bagel before getting some more writing done. I didn't have any other plans for the day. Not yet. Something I knew would please Matt to no end.

I'd just toasted a cheese bagel and added mocha creamer to my coffee when Mary Ann shuffled into the room. I set my breakfast down and hurried to her side. "You shouldn't walk around without help."

"I'm not an invalid." She plopped into a chair. "Your neighbors next door are running lawn equipment and woke me up. What time is it?"

"Eight."

She frowned. "Not too early." She rubbed her temples. "What are we doing today?"

I told her of my writing plans. "I need you to design a book cover."

"I can do that." Her face lit up. "I can't wait to see how this affects this loony tune who is out to get you."

"It's a dangerous game I'm playing, but I'm willing to help give them their moment of fame." I toasted a bagel for her and poured another cup of coffee. "I'm still a bit unsure of the motivation, though. It sounds a little crazy for someone to be so desperate for attention."

"Not so crazy. Lonely people sometimes take things to extremes." She bit into her bagel, her blue eyes glittering through the colorful bruises. "Look at history's serial killers. Something clicks in their brain, and they start killing people."

"You read too many of your brother's profiling books."

"Maybe." She shrugged. "But, I'm holding to the motivation we came up with. It makes as good sense as anything else."

"Okay, then who on our list is the most reclusive? The one most likely to be a desperate introvert?" I grabbed the notepad from my purse and set it in front of her.

She scanned the names. "Cheryl, Ms. Dillow, Tyler, or the old lady down the street. They all seem the most weird."

I laughed. "We can't accuse someone because they're weird."

"I don't think it's going to be someone across the street this time. What are the chances of that happening twice?"

True. I took a bite of my breakfast and stared out the window. I screamed and dropped my bagel, which Sadie immediately wolfed down. Tony Salazar stood on an overturned bucket and waved.

I yanked open the backdoor, sending the alarm squealing. "Hold on! Don't go anywhere!" I pointed a finger at him then rushed to turn off the alarm. Once peace had been restored, even if momentarily, I hurried outside. "What are you doing in my yard? You cost me my breakfast."

His smile faded. "My apologies, but I'm missing my cat."

My annoyance turned to concern. "When did you see it last?"

"Last night. We can't keep him inside. He dashes out the second the door is open and roams the neighborhood. Your dog wouldn't have eaten him, would she?"

"Definitely not unless she was covered in human food." I glanced toward the house where Mary Ann watched out the window. "I'm helping a friend recover from an accident, so can't really leave to help you search."

"Can I just take a look in your bushes?"

I nodded and headed back for house. "Oh, and this means I won't be able to help much with the Neighborhood Watch for a while."

"No problem. We'll take your turns, too. It will give us a chance to look for Bobo." He hopped off the bucket and scurried behind my junipers.

Some neighbors were just the best, and then others were like Ms. Henley or ... the Olseos. Mrs. Olson marched across the street and peered over my short fence. "That man has been snooping around your property all morning. If you weren't writing those smut novels of yours, you might have noticed.

I started to defend my work, again, and decided not to waste my time. She'd never read one of my books or she would know they were as clean as Easter sandals, marred with a bit of dust. Maybe she was confusing me with Sarah Thompson. "Thank you, but he's looking for his cat."

"He doesn't have a cat." She turned and stomped back to her house.

When I looked for Tony, he had disappeared.

"That was weird," I said reentering the house and setting the alarm. "Tony said he was looking for his cat, but Mrs. Olson said he didn't have one."

"She would know. That woman is the nosiest person I've ever met." Mary Ann had drawn squiggles all over our suspect list. "What do you think about setting up a meeting at the library to include Ms. Dillow and Cheryl? They're both involved with your books and are on our list. We could watch them together. See how they interact."

I closed the kitchen curtains. "That's a great idea." Why would Tony lie to me about owning a cat?

"Great. As your assistant, I'll get that worked out." She made a note on a fresh sheet of paper. "Maybe your mother can bring some snacks. I wish there was a way of getting all of our suspects to that meeting."

"I don't see how we can expect a young man

like Tyler to show up."

"Sure, we can! His mother is a fan. She doesn't drive. He'd have to bring her." Mary Ann tapped the pen against the paper. "What excuse do we use to involve her?"

"I know. I'll order a round of coffee drinks for Tyler to deliver and suggest he bring his mother so I can meet one of my readers." I sat at the table across from her. "If she doesn't drive, she fits our reclusive profile and will jump at the chance to get out of the house." I hoped. I also prayed she wouldn't bring a gun and go postal on the group, if she was the guilty party. A giant if.

"I need to get back to writing," I said. "I want this novella finished pronto. There's a lot riding on it."

"You could even slip at the meeting that it's almost ready."

"Great idea, just don't tell your brother. He'll put a stop to it all."

"Nah, him and Ryan will probably come to the meeting, too. They'll want to scope everyone out." She closed the notebook and headed for the living room. "I'll get my laptop and work on a cover at the table before taking a nap."

Exhaustion showed in her shoulders and the curve of her back. I hated the thought of her not getting the rest she needed because she helped me. "It can wait."

She nodded. "Maybe I'll take the laptop to bed with me. That way, I can fall asleep whenever I get the urge."

I watched as she headed to her room before entering my office. My spirits fell at the reminder of how much pain my dear friend was in. For so long I'd lived alone, keeping people at bay, not forming any solid relationships. Now, my family lived with me, I had a best friend, and a man I was quickly falling deeply in love with. So much had changed in such a short time and the weight of responsibility left me feeling a bit shackled.

Life, while boring and predictable six months ago, had left me as lonely as we believed my stalker to be. That hadn't sent me over the deep end into psychotic actions, though. I booted up my laptop. Ms. Dillow seemed nice enough to me and the 9-1-1 operator, Cheryl, was tickled to pieces to meet me. Tyler was a nice enough lad. None of them seemed like the aggressive, write-a-book-or-else, type of person. But, with nothing else to go on and no one else to add to my suspect list, I'd concentrate on them. Stranger things had happened.

My laptop glowed to life and showed I had several emails. My agent had received my message and after warning me about the implications of provoking a nutcase, wished me good luck and said it would help sell a ton of books. My thought exactly.

No email showed from my stalker. I'd gone almost a full day with no contact. I wasn't sure how to feel. Relieved? Worried? I bit the inside of my cheek. Was this some type of mind game designed to keep me on edge?

I peered out the window. Although my office sat on the second floor of my house, it wouldn't be impossible for someone to be watching. The skin on the back of my neck prickled. I grinned and gave a goofy wave, just in case. No sense in letting them know how terrified I was.

I settled back in my chair. Let them watch if

they were. All they'd see was a writer determined to finish their latest creation. On a whim, I grabbed a sheet of paper from the printer, wrote with a sharpie, and held the paper up to the window before God whispered in my ear that it might not be a wise choice. To make sure it stayed until my stalker could see it, I put a strip of tape on all four corners.

My note plainly stated, "Almost finished. I hope you like it. This book is dedicated to you!"

16

"Do you want to unveil the cover for *A Killer Plot* at the meeting?" Mary Ann slid a glossy photo across the kitchen table. "I think it's a killer."

I spewed coffee, marring the print.

"Good thing I printed off two." She set another at the opposite end from me.

"You're as evil as I am." I dabbed at the coffee splatters and studied the black background. *A Killer Plot*, the font signifying dripping blood, seemed suspended across the background. As if entering from an unseen room, a tiny figure walked from a cloud of wispy smoke. It carried a book in its hand.

"You are a genius, Mary Ann." No one would know from looking at the sinister cover the taunting story that resided within the pages. Instead, they'd think the book was as twisted as the cover portrayed

"Yes, let's unveil this tonight." All my suspects would be in one room at the library. I couldn't wait to gauge their reactions. Tonight could very well reveal the identity of my stalker.

"That's scary, kind of." Mom peered over our shoulders. "Help me load up the van, Stormi. The desserts are ready." She glanced from me to Mary Ann. "You two are up to something. I can tell. Oh, and Robert is coming tonight. He wants to help me serve the dessert, so I told Greta she didn't have to."

Great. One more possible suspect. It also wouldn't hurt for me to get to know Mom's boyfriend a bit better.

While Mary Ann slid the untarnished photo into a large bag, I hefted a box off the counter and headed out the front door. "Set the alarm."

Mom groaned. "This is such a nuisance."

By the time I had the box settled into the back of the van, the house was locked up tight. Mary Ann climbed into the back seat, leaving the front passenger seat for Mom. I slid behind the wheel. The party/meeting started in an hour. What had started as a mere way of getting a few suspects together had morphed into a celebration of my upcoming release. I grinned and turned the key in the ignition. Tonight would light some fireworks under someone's behind.

Mom and Mary Ann chattered as I made the ten minute drive to the library. Whenever Mom commented on how much fun the 'party' would be, I met Mary Ann's gaze in the rearview mirror. No one other than us knew the real reason for the get-together. Matt would have tried putting a stop to it immediately, and I didn't want Mom to act anything but natural.

I pulled the van as close to the library as possible. The conference room reserved for the night's events wasn't large by party standards, but this way, those in attendance would be forced into close proximity with each other and within hearing distance of me. I held high hopes for the evening. God willing, I'd gain valuable clues.

Ms. Dillow met us at the door. "Oh, this is exciting. Yes, it is. Imagine how another book by our local author will increase patronage and donations to our humble home for books." She cast a glance over her shoulder. "But there is an extremely bossy young woman trying to take over."

That would be Cheryl, if I made a guess. "She's in charge of the release party." I squeezed past, burdened down by cookies. "Which I won't need much longer. I've hired a literary assistant."

"Oh?" Ms. Dillow trotted to keep up with me.

"Me." Mary Ann smiled under her bruises and hurried to hold the conference room door open. "I'm the one who planned this little shindig."

"Then you'd better get in there and stop that woman from messing up your plans." Ms. Dillow stormed past us, clearly upset at our news.

Mary Ann and I exchanged delighted glances and hurried into the room. Sure enough, Cheryl had taken over. Balloons and streamers in pink and black hung everywhere. A bit overdone for a simple unveiling, but it was no secret how excited she was about the release of another book. I batted a balloon out of the way with my head and headed for the table set up at one end of the room.

"We won't be able to see everything that's going on with all this stuff." Mary Ann wrapped her hand in a streamer and yanked, pulling it free from the tape.

"I worked hard on that!" Cheryl cut another piece of bubble gum pink streamer.

"You didn't have to go to so much trouble," I said. "It's a simple meeting. There won't be a large crowd here." My eyes widened, catching a glimpse of Mom planting a quick kiss on Robert's lips. A balloon drifted, cutting off my view.

"I only want to show you what I'm capable of."
She glared and stomped away.

Mary Ann and I shared another glance, and
grinned. Everything was progressing exactly as planned.

Tyler, and a woman who didn't look old enough
to be his mother, approached the table, a tray with
blended coffees in their hands. A bright blue dress did
its best to hold the woman's amplified bosom in place,
and failed. The flesh oozing over the neckline jiggled like
jelly. Five inch heels caused the woman to tower over
my short frame, bringing her 'girls' to my eye level.
Heavily frosted hair hid what few gray hairs she might
possess, and sparkling green eyes twinkled as she set
the tray down and rounded the table to give me a hug.

Smothering in perfumed flesh, I held my breath
and latched on to a glimpse of Matt entering the room.
"It's nice to meet you, Mrs...?"

"Norma Winston." She held me at arm's length.
"There's no mister and never has been. Why lock myself
into a relationship that will only go sour in a few years?
Life is too short. A woman is meant to take what she
wants." She put an arm around Tyler's shoulders. He
rolled his eyes. "Take my son, here. He doesn't plan on
settling down, do you, sweetie? People will always
disappoint. Always. Oh."

Oops. She caught a glimpse of my man. "Now,
that is delicious." She set the tray she carried on the
table and hurried away.

"Sorry about that," Tyler said. "My mother is a
bit ... hard to take for some people. She's ruthless,
unscrupulous, you name it."

"She seems very ... friendly." I chose the
smallest coffee, took a sip, and then set it on a table
behind me. After too many late nights writing, I looked

forward to a good night's sleep.

He snorted. "That's a nice way of putting it. I'll serve the coffee." He moved around the room, tray in hand, letting those in attendance choose their beverage of choice.

By now, my entire family, Cheryl, Ms. Dillow, Tyler and his mother, myself, Mary Ann, Robert, Matt, Ryan, and a few curious strangers filled the room and nibbled on Mom's delicious cookies. Let the games begin. My stalker was here, I knew it. Excitement and apprehension skipped up my backbone.

I retrieved my coffee, and sipped. After draining the cup, I tossed it into a nearby trashcan overflowing with cups, napkins, popped balloons, and oleander flowers.

I squared my shoulders and clapped my hands. "May I have your attention, please? You may have to crowd close because of the decorations. I don't want anyone to miss the big reveal." Once everyone was within sight of the table I stood behind, I continued. "As you know, I've called anyone involved with the soon-to-be-released next novel of mine. I've recently received the cover art and am thrilled to be able to present it to you … my biggest fans, and those who have made this possible," I whipped off the napkin covering the photo. "the cover to *A Killer Plot*."

Silence filled the room. I scanned the faces. In front of the crowd stood a stony-faced Cheryl and a granite-faced Ms. Dillow. Matt's eyes widened, Ryan didn't know what to say, and my sister held a hand over her mouth to hide a grin. No doubt she had figured out exactly what I was trying to do. Mom looked as irritated as she used to when I had been up to no good as a child.

"That," Ms. Dillow pointed at the photo. "Does

not look anything like the first book."

Cheryl moved closer. "Isn't this supposed to be the second book in a series? Shouldn't they look the same?"

"The figure on the cover looks deformed," Dakota stated, shoving a cookie in his mouth. "The cover is awesome in being suspenseful looking, but the person is almost cartoonish. Is that the look you were going for?"

Bless you, my nephew. You are the smartest tack in the room.

Norma crossed her arms, making her bosom even more pronounced. "Is this a joke? Where's the real cover?"

"This is it." I kept my grin firmly in place and avoided the steely-eyed gaze of Matt. I knew he'd figured out my trick in quick time.

"What's this second book about anyway?" Ms. Dillow asked. "I want to know this instant."

"It's about a bumbling email stalker who, while attempting to harm the protagonist, actually only makes their life more difficult. The stalker's life, not the main character's. I've modeled it after some recent events." I draped the napkin back over the photo. "So, yes, the cover does depict the story; suspense with slap-stick humor." I stepped back to watch where the cards would fall.

"How is that supposed to help the library?" Ms. Dillow asked.

"I can't plan a release party for something so awful," Cheryl said.

"I'm not sure I want to read any more of your books," Norma said. "I muddle through, even though they have no sex, because the story is so entertaining.

But a bumbling email stalker? That's almost offensive in comparison to what you usually write."

"I understand all of your concerns, and am more than willing to listen to each of you, privately, any time you wish. As the author, it is my prerogative to change my stories."

"No!" Ms. Dillow stomped her foot. "As the author, it is up to you to satisfy your readers."

Heads nodded around the room.

Mom stepped up to the table. "There are more cookies and snacks on the side table to enjoy while you discuss the new cover." She turned to me, and hissed, "Are you crazy?"

"A little bit." I smiled and high-fived Mary Ann.

"Ah, I get it." Mom nodded. "You're trying to draw out your stalker."

"And putting an even bigger target on your back." Matt took me by the arm and pulled me from the room. Outside, he rubbed his hands down his face. "Do you mind telling me what all that was about?"

"My new book cover." I choked off a giggle.

His eyes glittered in the light of a street lamp. "While the cover is very interesting, I also recognize my sister's handiwork. That is the cover she drew in Junior High art class. She never could do people very well. What are you doing?"

"It's not an original? Oh, well. It won't matter."

"It is an original. She drew it herself. Stop trying to change the subject." He leaned against the post.

"You're right." I sighed. "I'm trying to draw out the bad guy or woman, as I suspect it may be. Have you noticed, except for Mary Ann's accident and near-escape from meeting Jesus, we have no dead bodies? Women don't like things messy."

"Ms. Henley didn't seem to have a problem."

"True, but she was protecting her son. Not that I excuse her actions, but I've read numerous times about how mothers can be driven to extremes when their children are threatened. I still say my stalker is a woman."

"One of the women here?" He glanced toward the building.

"Yes."

"They've all checked out."

"That only means they've never committed a crime before. We need to see whether they've had any stressors in their life. Something to set them over the edge."

"Stop thinking like a detective and start thinking like a woman who wants to stay alive."

"I do want to stay alive." I stepped closer, inviting him to take me into his arms. "But staying out here with you isn't allowing me to eavesdrop in there."

"Do you care about me, Stormi?"

"Very much."

"Then why are you trying so hard to kill me?"

Something rustled in the oleander bushes behind me. Matt yanked me behind him. "Who's there?"

I never could understand why people asked that question. If I were hiding and intended ill toward someone, I wouldn't announce myself.

"It's me." Cherokee skulked from the bushes, followed by Tyler. "Don't tell Mom, okay? We weren't doing anything wrong."

Poor Sarah would be so heartbroken. She had someone else picked out for Tyler, at least in her latest smut book. "If you weren't doing anything wrong, then why were you hiding? You do know that plant is poisonous, right?"

"Because Mom gets freaked out every time I have a boyfriend, and yes, I know its poisonous, but we aren't eating it."

Well, that explains why Tyler was so eager to accept my invitation to deliver coffee to my get-together. "I'll try talking to your mother if she gets wind of this. For now, you two get back inside."

I tried running back through my mind as to what, exactly, Matt and I had discussed. If Cherokee and Tyler had been in there the whole time, they could have heard something damaging that Tyler could then repeat to his mother and thwart my plan.

17

An hour later, Matt and I sat around the table with Mary Ann and Ryan. Mary Ann's eyelids drooped, but she refused to go to bed despite the clock chiming nine o'clock. "I don't want to miss anything."

"Then let's move to the living room so you can fall asleep on the sofa if you want." Matt helped her to her feet.

"Anyone want coffee?" I asked.

"I do. It's my turn to keep watch tonight," Ryan said.

"It's always your turn." I measured coffee grounds. "You'll keel over from exhaustion if you aren't careful. Then, how am I going to get you to date my sister." I grinned.

"You want me to date Angela?" His dark eyes narrowed. "Why? She's as white as white can be and I'm—"

"I know what you are. That doesn't matter to me or my sister. I've seen the way you two look at each other." I pushed the button on the coffee pot. "All I care about is that she finds a good man, and you're a good man."

He put one large hand over his heart. "I'm touched." He pointed. "Shouldn't you have a pot under that?"

"Oh." I'd forgotten the pot. Now a fragrant stream of coffee ran across the countertop and onto the floor. "Let me get this cleaned up, and I'll join y'all in the other room." Idiot. I swiped my forearm across my forehead. It sure was hot in the house for October. My stomach cramped. Maybe I was the one who needed to lie down.

Instead, I muddled through, made the coffee, and then joined the others. Matt leaped up to take the tray from me. "Are you all right?"

I shook my head. "I feel like I might be coming down with the flu. Let's discuss tonight, so Mary Ann and I can both lie down. We were going to discuss stressors."

"I mentioned that we were more concerned with Ms. Dillow, Cheryl, and Tyler's mother," Mary Ann explained. "Since the three are your biggest so-called fans."

"Janet Dillow is being let go at the end of the year," Ryan read from a notepad in his lap. "The library is cutting back due to lack of funds. Cheryl Isaacson takes care of her aging, very overweight mother, and spends a large portion of her paycheck on reading material. Norma Winston is in foreclosure. All three women have things going on in their lives that would cause them to snap. The only thing that makes me hesitant is that no one has reacted violently."

"Hey, someone cut my brakes." Mary Ann threw a pillow at him.

"True, but usually when someone snaps, they choose a more aggressive form of murder."

I groaned and pressed a sofa pillow against my abdomen. "Not everyone reacts the same way."

Matt placed the back of his hand against my cheek. "You're burning up."

"It's kind of hot in here."

"No, it isn't."

"I'm going to throw up." I leaped to my feet and raced to the restroom. I lost my cookies, literally, in the toilet before falling to my knees. This was no ordinary flu.

"How long have you felt like this?" Matt helped me to my feet, sat me on the edge of the tub, and reached for a clean washcloth.

"An hour, maybe?"

"I'm taking you to the hospital." He wet the rag, placed it across my forehead and scooped me into his arms. "Stay with Mary Ann," he told Ryan. "I think Stormi has been poisoned."

"What?" Convulsions seized my body, whether from cold or from fear, I couldn't say. Poison? The oleanders. "Matt, there were oleander blossoms in the trash can at the party. The can right next to my coffee."

"Call an ambulance." He dashed back to the bathroom and sat me on the side of the tub again. "Throw up again."

"I don't need to."

"Stick your finger down your throat."

"You're scaring me." I sagged to the floor. My heart raced. "I feel like I'm going to have a heart attack."

"Tell the operator that we think it's oleander poisoning," Matt yelled down the hall. "And don't talk to Cheryl Isaacson."

I doubled over, the pain so intense, perspiration poured down my face and back. I didn't want to die. Not like this. I gripped Matt's hand. "I'm going to pass out."

"No, you're not." He sat next to me, wrapping his strong arms around me. "Stay with me, Stormi."

"And you thought I was trying to kill you." I tried to laugh off my fear and pain, instead the sound came out as more of a strangled cough. "Back at the library. Remember? When you asked if I cared about you?"

"I remember." He rested his chin on the top of my head.

Sirens filled the air. Matt lifted me again and rushed to meet them. My hero, not wanting to waste the seconds it would take for the paramedics to come into the house. He laid me on a gurney where someone injected me with a needle. "I hope that's a cardiac depressant," I said, "because my heart is going faster than a falling star."

I closed my eyes, giving into the darkness.

When I woke, Mom and Matt were both snoozing in chairs beside my bed. My mouth tasted bitter and was as dry as if filled with cotton. Relieved that I still breathed, I pushed the button next to me and raised my bed. "Hey."

Matt's eyes popped open. "Hey, yourself. How do you feel?"

"Thirsty. Was it oleander?"

"We think so. At least the treatment worked."

"No one else got sick," Mom said. "So, it wasn't the cookies. You must have drank it in your coffee."

I thought back. I'd taken a coffee out of habit when Tyler's mother presented the tray and set it behind me. Anyone could have tampered with it while grabbing a cookie. My heart skipped a beat. Someone had actually tried to kill me. No longer was my stalker someone who stayed in the background. They'd taken a giant step forward. "My plan is working."

"Too bad your brain isn't." Mom crossed her arms. "Antagonizing a psycho is never a good idea."

"I have to agree with Ann on this one." Matt sighed. "If we hadn't stayed to discuss what happened at the party, you would have died in your sleep."

"But, I didn't, so now what?"

"Ryan is interrogating everyone at the library. While the Winstons brought the coffee, you said you set yours down, thus making it accessible to anyone."

"I need my laptop." Maybe the attempted killer sent me a message.

"I thought you would." Mom pulled my laptop from her shoulder bag.

Sure enough, an email awaited, and not a happy one. I read, "I hope you liked your coffee, not that I'm sure you'll even get to read this. Oleander stalks make wonderful coffee stirrers. Oh, and if you are alive to read this, take your note out of your office window and make a new cover for the book. Heaven can't help you if I don't approve of the cover or the story."

"Oh, we're a greedy little bugger, aren't we?" I closed the laptop. "I'm not changing a thing."

"You're increasing the risk to yourself." Tears welled in Mom's eyes. "Six months ago, I was as gung ho as you, but then, someone hadn't tried to poison you."

"No, they just took the entire family at gunpoint."

"After we knew who the killer was."

"Mom, does that really matter?"

"Yes. Not knowing is way worse."

"Ladies," Matt interrupted. "It's going to be fine. I won't be leaving Stormi or Mary Ann alone again.

I'll be sleeping on your sofa until this is over, and Detective Koontz will do the leg work."

"You'll be bored out of your mind." I slapped the mattress, hitting the button that lowered my bed, and jerked back.

"I'm never bored when I'm with you," he said. "It's impossible."

"Mom, I want you and Angela to take the kids and go to the cabin." Although I knew her answer, I couldn't help but ask again.

"And leave you and Matthew in the house unsupervised? What kind of a mother would that make me?"

"Mary Ann is there. Please."

She shook her head. "No, we're in this together. Oh, I'm as crazy as you are. If I didn't have a business to run, I know I'd be right there in the thick of things like you and Mary Ann."

I was glad she had the store to keep her busy. The less people involved the better. I met Matt's gaze. Worry lines radiated from the corners of his eyes. I'd tried to send him on his way. Even though my heart would have broken, it might have been the best thing. Now, his sister was injured, he had taken leave from a job he loved, and I'd almost died. What if he was next and couldn't escape the fate his sister and I had?

"Good afternoon." A man in a white doctor's coat entered the room. "It's good to see you awake. Are you ready to go home?"

"Afternoon? How long have I been here?" I glanced at Mom and Matt.

"Since last night," the doctor answered. "We treated you and let you rest. You can go home now." He handed me papers to sign. "Try not to put any more plants in your mouth, all right?"

I nodded, feeling very much like a child, even though ingesting the poison hadn't been by choice or ignorance. I swung my legs over the side of the bed as Matt followed the doctor from the room. "Mom."

"Yes?" She handed me my clothes. "If you're going to bring up me leaving again, I'm going to smack you."

My shoulders slumped as I slipped my legs into my jeans. If she insisted on staying, I'd have to continue working hard to keep the stalker's attention fixed on me and me only. I also wouldn't put anything into my mouth unless it never left my sight. When I discovered the identity of my stalker, we were going to rumble. For now, I needed to get home and finish the novella. Fireworks were going to explode when the book hit the digital book shelves.

"What are you cooking up in that mind of yours?" Mom handed me my shoes.

"I'm planning on a time to meet my admirer. It's going to be very special."

18

Loud voices woke me the next morning. I put the pillow over my head. It worked until Sadie leaned on the windowsill and barked. "Ugh." I threw the pillow at her feet and climbed out of bed. "What is so critical that you must bark at seven a.m.?"

I parted the sheer drapes over my window. Matt stood on the sidewalk between an angry Tony Salazar and an equally annoyed Mark Wood. Their wives stood behind their husbands, arms crossed. Tony might be a small man, but the waves of indignation radiating from him were giant sized. I raised the window more than the couple of inches I'd left it open last night and leaned out.

"Gentlemen, we can resolve the situation without violence." Matt held out his hands.

"That man … made wolf whistles at my wife," Tony said.

"And I told you it wasn't me." Mark shook his head. "Have you seen *my* wife? Seriously, dude."

"So, now my wife isn't good enough for you?" Tony took a step forward, fists clenched. "Why'd you follow us here anyway? If you would have stayed in the old neighborhood, we wouldn't be having this conversation."

Oooh, things just got interesting. I leaned out further. My neighbors knew each other from before. What was their connection? I'd take any distraction from my stalker problems. I was still reeling from the fact I'd almost died. Of course, it wasn't the first time, but it hadn't lost its ... non-thrill.

"Back off, Shorty, or I'll let these fine neighbors know all about you." Mark grinned like a shark. "That's right. I know all about your sordid past, you little computer geek."

"Oh, yeah? Well, I know what that tattoo on your arm means. You aren't innocent, either."

Tattoo? I could barely make out what looked like a counter. The sort you'd see on a website, maybe.

Frustration outlined Matt's shoulders. Poor thing. If he left, the two might come to blows, if he stayed, he lost valuable time searching for our elusive stalker. I pulled away from the window.

Secrets abounded, as usual, in Oak Meadow Estates. What if I'd been looking in the wrong direction? It was quite possible the women I suspected were innocent. But what about the poison? Neither of my neighbors had been at the library. That I knew of. I leaned back out the window, balancing on my stomach. The men had moved, almost disappearing around the corner. I couldn't see Matt, but could barely hear loud whispering. I was missing something important. I knew it!

Sadie woofed low in her throat and planted both paws against my cotton-clad behind. I shrieked and reached for the branch of the oak tree outside my window. I grabbed hold, hanging like a poor kitty I'd seen on a poster once, except I didn't have claws, and didn't like being in a tree. I glanced toward the window where Sadie appeared to be grinning, her pink tongue hanging out.

"Help! Matt!" I so didn't want to be discovered, but if help didn't arrive soon, I'd be in a crumpled mess on the ground.

"What in heaven's name are you doing up there?" Matt's called out. "Hold on. Let me find a ladder."

"I don't have a ladder."

"I do." Mark Wood hurried away. I could have sworn he was laughing.

"Were you spying?" Matt asked, his handsome face split with a grin.

"Yes. Sadie knocked me out the window."

I thanked the Good Lord I'd worn cotton shorts and a tee shirt to bed instead of a nightgown. I gave the neighbors plenty to talk about without showing them my underwear. "My hands are getting sweaty." I slipped and screamed. I shivered in the chilly October morning, further increasing my chance of falling.

"Kick your leg up and over the next branch."

"Are you crazy?" That branch had to be at least six inches away, which in my predicament seemed more like six feet. If I moved, my grip would loosen more.

"Why is Stormi in a tree?" Mary Ann joined her brother on the lawn. "Was she being too nosey?"

"Of course, she was." Matt laughed. "The ladder is coming. Of course, if you wished, you could just let go. Your feet are only about four feet off the ground."

Seriously, I was going to fall while they laughed. Wait. Four feet? I glanced down. Sure enough, my weight had bent the limb almost to the ground. I let go and landed like a cat on my paws, or hands and feet, rather. "Why didn't you say so sooner?" I brushed off my hands. "I was terrified."

He shrugged. "It was more fun watching you kick."

"You're evil." I stomped past him and into the house. A terrifying experience such as that warranted coffee. Lots of it.

"Hey, Stormi." Ryan held the door open. "Nice to have you hanging around." He guffawed, the big oaf.

"Shut up." I banged my shoulder against him as I entered the house. Instead of heading straight for the kitchen, I went back to my room. I'd be able to function better in the face of ridicule if I weren't wearing my pajamas.

After slipping on a pair of jeans and a long-sleeved tee shirt, I joined the others in the kitchen where Matt was already brewing coffee. I mumbled a good morning and snagged a glazed doughnut from the box on the table. "Who brought these?"

"I did," Ryan said. "You know what they say about cops and doughnuts."

"Is that actually true?" My eyes widened.

He laughed. "No, I just like doughnuts. Maybe they'll sweeten your mood."

"Hmmm." I bit into one, my mind already racing on to what I wanted to do that day. My options were: dig into the secrets of my neighbors or focus on one of my suspects. I didn't have a reason to ask Ms. Dillow about library cutbacks and wasn't sure whether it was common knowledge that she was being let go. I settled on purchasing a cake from Mom and taking it to Cheryl at home. I could say I'd heard of her ill mother and wanted to ease her burden a bit.

"Does anyone know whether Cheryl Isaacson

works today?"

Matt turned, mugs of coffee in each hand. "She works nights, why?"

"I'm thinking of paying her a condolence visit." I accepted one of the mugs. "I'll ask her whether there is anything I can help her with, since she thinks she's in charge of my book release party."

"You want to snoop around her house." His brow lowered.

"Of course, I do." I held up a hand to ward off his protests. "I know you're going to want to accompany me, and I won't argue. The only thing I ask is that you stay in the car and out of sight. You can put a wire on me if you want, but I doubt she'll say anything of value with you along."

He peered at me over the rim of his cup. After taking a long sip, he nodded. "I can live with that ... if you wear a wire and carry a Taser."

"I can do that." My stomach fluttered. I'd really thought I'd have to argue my way to Cheryl's. "Thank you."

"I want to come." Mary Ann snagged a doughnut. "As your literary assistant, it's part of my job."

"No, it isn't."

"Well, since I took off work until Monday so I don't scare the kiddos with my bruises, I don't have anything else to do. Besides, there's safety in numbers, or so they say. It didn't help you at the library, though, did it? Don't eat anything while we're there, even if she offers you something."

I wanted her to stop talking. From the red spots on Matt's cheeks, I could tell he was having second thoughts about letting me go.

"Yes, mother. I want to stop and buy some kind of a dessert. Then, it will be safe to eat it."

"Let's take the mini-van." Matt set his cup down. "Ryan and I can hide easier that way."

"Mom has it."

"We'll get it when we're there."

"Right." And I was the mystery writer. That poison must have short-circuited something in my brain. Usually, I was right on top of things.

"I'll get the wire." Ryan hefted his bulk out of the chair and went outside, returning five minutes later with a small clip. "Hook this to your—" He waved his hand around my chest area.

"Got it." I took the small microphone and went into the bathroom. I hooked it to my bra strap, as close to my mouth as I could get it. The only problem with that spot was that it left a bump in my tee shirt. "Hey, will you still be able to hear me if I put this in my cleavage?" I poked my head out the door.

"Yes!" Matt called back.

Problem solved. I did my business while in there, brushed my teeth, and five minutes later, purse over my arm, I was ready to go. "Should we do a sound check?"

"We could hear you fumbling in the bathroom." Ryan ducked his head.

Good grief. Color me red and call me embarrassed. Avoiding their amused glances, I headed to the van, Mary Ann hot on my heels. "I do manage to get myself into ridiculous situations."

"You wouldn't be Stormi if you didn't." She giggled and got in the backseat of her brother's car. "That's what makes being around you so much fun."

"Your brother doesn't think so."

"He's still here, isn't he?"

True. I clicked my seatbelt into place as the men entered the car.

Matt met my gaze in the rearview mirror. "Are you sure you want to do this?"

I nodded. "We need to start marking people off the suspect list. She may check out in your police computers, but there is still a cloud of suspicion hanging over her head. Maybe this visit will dispel that."

"You're in the wrong line of work." He started the car and backed from the driveway. "You would make a good detective with the way your mind works. If not for the fact you tend to rush into things."

Being a good detective was just as necessary when writing a mystery. How else would everything fall into place and make sense? Just because I didn't carry a badge, didn't mean I wasn't a detective, right? I was a romantic mystery detecting author.

Matt pulled in front of Heavenly Bakes. While the others waited in the car, I rushed into the store. "Mom, I need something delicious. Something that will make someone comfortable and talkative." I pushed through a small swinging door she'd installed and into her work area.

"I've some delightful lemon cake bars." She wiped her hands on her apron. "Who are you going to see?"

"Cheryl Isaacson."

"Ah, she likes chocolate." Mom pulled a tray of tiny cake bites, decorated with pastel flowers, from the refrigerator. "She bought a few of these last week and practically swooned."

"I'll take a dozen, plus one." I popped one in my mouth. While they were technically cakes, the texture was so moist it practically dissolved in my mouth. "How much?"

"Free, if you stop by and tell me how it went." She frowned. "That's the only drawback to owning a business. I have to spend a lot of time here and can't go snooping with you."

"After a while, maybe." I looked to where Greta folded boxes. "Once you're settled and have enough stock and people to help you, you can take off. Oh, and I need to borrow the van."

Her face brightened. She grabbed a set of keys from beside the computer. "That's right. Greta already does all the baking. I decorate. We actually have time to experiment with recipes. Soon, I'm going to hire a counter girl who will also take orders." She hugged me. "I can't thank you enough for making this possible."

Tears filled my eyes. "I'm glad to help, Mom." Being a silent partner wasn't bad at all. "I've got to go. I promise to let you know how it went."

"Just stay alive, sweetie."

19

The others waited beside the van when I stepped back outside.

"Did you bring us anything?" Ryan leaned over the box, his nostrils twitching.

"Nope. Sorry. I'll get something on the way back." I twirled the keys. "We have to return the van anyway. It will be our reward for a job well done."

"You had something." He pointed to the corner of his mouth. "You carry the evidence."

I licked the crumbs off my mouth, and grinned. "Prove it."

He eyed the box hungrily and climbed in the back of the van. Matt did the same, leaving the front for myself and Mary Ann. "I hope someone had the foresight to look up her address."

Ryan handed me a slip of paper. "Not the best neighborhood, but since we're in the van, you should be okay."

I almost asked him to define 'not the best neighborhood' but decided it couldn't be too bad. I was wrong.

We pulled in front of a one-story ranch-style house badly in need of a new roof and paint job. What once might have been a cheery yellow was now a dingy washed out lemon color. In the yard next door, three male teenagers, basketball shorts hanging down around the bottom of their butt cheeks, stared. I was doubly glad Matt and Ryan were with us. The two provided a great deterrent for anyone intending us harm.

The men climbed out the back of the van and leaned against the doors, staying out of sight of the house, but in plain sight of the belligerent youths. I dared the youngsters to make a move toward me or Mary Ann. Our bodyguards would be all over them like angry flies on sugar.

I clutched the box of delicacies and approached the porch, Mary Ann glued to my side. The curtains were drawn tight. The doorbell hung by its wires. "Do you think she really lives here?"

"Matt said she did." Mary Ann pressed closer. "Knock. I don't trust that doorbell. You could get shocked."

"Hey, pretty thing!" One of the young men took a couple of steps in our direction. "You look like your man did a number on you. You belong to the big boy over there?"

Mary Ann shook her head and held a finger to her lips. "If he doesn't be quiet, he's going to alert Cheryl to Matt and Ryan."

I rapped on the door as hard as I could, praying Cheryl would answer quickly. When seconds passed with no answer, I banged again.

"What is so important—" She yanked the door open. "Stormi. Oh, wow."

I grinned and held out the box. "May we come in?"

Her face fell. "I'm not really receiving company."

"I've brought sweets. Your favorite, my mother said."

She licked her lips. "Forgive the mess." She grabbed the box and stepped aside.

Mess was an understatement. The smell met us at the door. Empty food containers and dirty dishes added to the clutter of millions of items. Clothes, garbage, and household items filled the house, leaving a narrow path to traverse. One armchair sat in front of a twenty inch television. I breathed through my nose and fought to keep my smile in place.

"I heard you spend a lot of your time caring for your aging mother." I turned to face Cheryl as if visiting the home of a hoarder was a common thing. "I came to see how I could help ease your burden."

"Why?" Cheryl popped a treat in her mouth.

"You've done so much for me." I took a deep breath, instantly fighting back a gag. Mary Ann's eyes looked as if they'd pop out of her head.

Cheryl cocked her head. "Come on into the kitchen. I'll get you something to drink."

Mary Ann shook her head violently behind Cheryl's back. I mouthed that I wouldn't drink a thing. Anything I put in my mouth was liable to come back up anyway.

We followed Cheryl down the maze. A box beside the easy chair caught my attention.

I stopped and gazed upon more than twenty of my latest mystery novel. Balanced on the arm of the chair was a rubber stamp with my signature. I pocketed the stamp, pulled my tee shirt down to cover the bulge, and hurried to catch up with the other two. Since my agent had refused to send Cheryl a case of free books, the woman must have forked out a pretty penny for them.

The kitchen was worse than the living room and the smell twice as bad. "Is your mother home?"

"She never comes out of her room." Cheryl ate another treat. "She's too fat to get around. It's time for her bath, though. Would you like to help with that?"

Oh, God, no. I needed to think of something fast. "Maybe I could fix her lunch while you enjoy your treat?"

Cheryl swiped a pile of magazines off a kitchen chair and motioned Mary Ann to sit. She eyed the stained wood with distaste and perched on the edge. "There's cans of soup on top of the fridge. You'll have to use the microwave. The stove is covered with stuff. I keep meaning to clean up, but Mom takes so much of my time."

"What did you think of the party the other night?" I reached over a pile of junk to grab a can of vegetable soup and dislodged a pile of rotten smelling rags.

"It was all right," she said. "But the librarian kept butting her nose into my job. Not to mention your friend here. If you wanted to hire an assistant, you could have hired me."

"Hey," Mary Ann protested. "I'm her best friend and the sister of her boyfriend."

"No offense."

Can in hand, I went in search of a relatively clean bowl. "Why don't you hire a crew to help you clear some of this out?"

"It's Mom's house, and she says no. What she says goes." Cheryl sighed. "It won't matter for much longer anyway. I'm pretty sure the city will condemn the house."

"Where will you go?" I dumped the soup into a plastic bowl and stuck it into a microwave so peppered with unidentified spatters that it was bound to help season the meal.

"An apartment somewhere. I have a little side job selling used books. It brings in a nice bit of cash to buy me the little things I love, like these treats."

The rubber stamp weighed heavy in my pocket. The woman was forging my signature and selling copies of my book as signed by the author. While flattered that people would pay extra for signed copies, I didn't like her taking what belonged to me. And where was she getting the books? I should have taken a closer look. I had a feeling she was buying used copies and selling them as new, which might be a crime, but it didn't mean she was my stalker. Now, that I thought of it, I couldn't see her buying a case of new books.

I didn't see a computer anywhere, which made me question whether she was my stalker.

"So, by helping with my mother, does that mean you'll come by regularly to allow me some time out of the house?" Cheryl balanced the box on top of a pile of laundry. "Because the only other time I get out is when I'm at work. Mom fends for herself then. She really doesn't need a nurse."

The microwave dinged. I found a pot holder and removed the bowl. "Oh, then I guess we'll just pop in once in a while to visit with you." That wouldn't be for a very long time if I could help it. I felt as if we were breathing toxic fumes, and I hadn't found out anything relevant to the case.

"How computer savvy are you?" I asked. "I'm thinking of setting up a newsletter."

"I'm very techie. In fact, I went to college for

computers."

Interesting, but still didn't label her a stalker. Maybe I should flat out ask her whether she was my stalker. "Which room is your mother's?"

"Down the hall. Last room on the right. Her name is Rose."

As carefully as I could without tripping over something, I headed down the hall, peeking in rooms as I went. Surprisingly enough, the first bedroom I came to was spotless. The bathroom would require me wearing a Hezmet suit before I'd enter.

Rose's room contained nothing more than the largest woman I'd ever seen, reclining on a mattress that filled the small space, a table like the ones used in hospitals, and a television mounted on the wall. Obviously, the home's residents believed in keeping where they slept clean.

"Rose? I'm Stormi Nelson. I've brought you lunch." I set the bowl on the table.

"I know who you are." Dark eyes peered from the folds of her face. "My daughter is obsessed with you."

Chills skipped up my spine. "How so?"

"Didn't you see the boxes of books? She buys them anywhere she can get them for a buck or two and resells them at full value. She's nothing more than a crook and a slob." She thinks because I can't leave my room that I don't know what she's done to my house, but I have someone who comes and checks on my health once a week and I've been informed."

"Why aren't you in a nursing home?"

Tears sparkled in her eyes. "Cheryl refuses."

"Would you like to go?"

"Yes. Very much." She grasped my hand. "Can

you make it happen?"

"I know someone who can." I patted her shoulder. "It was nice to meet you, Rose. I look forward to seeing you again when I can breathe properly."

She laughed, the sound so like the giggles of a small child that I couldn't help but laugh along. I think Rose will be someone I enjoy visiting. "I'll have someone stop by and help you as soon as possible."

"Don't leave yet. Sit while I eat."

I had the feeling Cheryl left her mother alone a lot. "Will you want something else?"

"I'd like some of those treats you brought, but I doubt my stingy daughter will share."

"I'll bring you your own box."

She grinned. "Make sure you do. Food is my only comfort, if you can't tell."

"I know of someone who can bring you the greatest comfort."

"You're talking about God, aren't you?" She shook her head. "I know, but this old body of mine can't get to church anymore. That's another reason I want out of this place. I feel like God can't find me among all the junk."

"He knows you're here, sweetie." I sat back while she slurped her soup, grateful I'd come, even if I'd come under false pretenses. It warmed my heart to know I'd lessened someone's loneliness, if only for a while. "Rose, you said Cheryl was obsessed with me. She wouldn't be so far off the deep end that she'd stalk me, would she?"

Rose's hand paused halfway from the bowl to her mouth. "I don't think so. I'm not sure how she would find the time."

"I don't mean physically stalk, more like on a

computer."

"That's a possibility. That television of hers has the capabilities of a computer."

I nodded, my shoulders slumping. If someone could treat their mother the way Cheryl treated hers, it wasn't hard to imagine them trying to kill someone who wasn't a member of their family.

"You almost done in there?" Cheryl called from the front of the house. "Don't let Mom monopolize your time."

I sighed. "I'll be back, Rose. I promise, and I'll bring reinforcements."

"Be careful, then. My girl can carry a grudge like no other."

20

One down, two more to go. By the time I'd collected a very disgusted Mary Ann from Cheryl's clutches, Matt had already called social services, thanks to the wire in my bra. By the time they got there, Cheryl was stomping mad and had resigned as my book release planner. So sad. I wasn't sure I'd ever get over the rejection.

"So," I turned to Mary Ann. "What kind of ploy can we use on Norma Winston?"

"Haven't you angered enough people today?" Matt closed my door, then jogged around to the driver's side. Since there was no more reason for Matt to stay where Cheryl couldn't see him, he wanted to drive.

"I want this over with," I said as he slid behind the wheel. "That means meeting with Norma and Ms. Dillow, preferably not at the same time. What do we know about Norma?"

"She's losing her home," Mary Ann. "At least that's the rumor through the grapevine. Not sure how that relates to her being your stalker, though. There's no money in stalking, and she needs money."

"You're right. It doesn't make any sense for her to be the one harassing me." I drummed my fingers on the armrest. Could it be that simple? Was it possible I'd narrowed my suspects down to two? I needed to focus on motive.

I pulled the rubber signature stamp from my pocket. "Cheryl has been forging my signature and selling lots of my books for top dollar. Why? To make money. If she was against putting her mother in a nursing home, why the dire need for cash?"

Matt pulled the van onto the highway. "Maybe she has an addiction we don't know about?"

"Yeah, chocolate," Mary Ann said. "She didn't offer me a single piece of those little cakes. Not that I could have eaten with that smell, but still. It really smelled as if something had died in there."

"I've called to have a clean-up crew empty out the house. The city said either Cheryl cleans it up or she'll have to move."

That still didn't give her a legitimate reason to stalk me. I gnawed my bottom lip. I couldn't figure out a proper motive for Ms. Dillow, either. So, the library was cutting back and she could be out of a job. How did I fall into that?

"While you three have been tossing ideas back and forth," Ryan said, "I've been doing a bit of research on Norma Winston. She's been picked up twice for solicitation and once for shoplifting. Her Facebook page says she's a writer of fan fiction. Guess who her model is?"

"Me." Now, we had a motive. "What's the name of her book?"

"Anything."

"That's it?"

"Yep."

Not very creative. I ordered the ebook version on my cell phone and read drivel worse than Sarah Thompson's fumbling sex stories. While the basic idea resembled my novel in a vague sort of way, there was enough sex scenes between the characters to stun the Pope into a coma. Still, Norma had several five star reviews and a high author ranking. She could very well be my stalker, especially if her writing depended on mine. I needed to stop by the coffee shop and talk to Tyler. I might as well create as much havoc in one day as possible, and get it out of the way.

"I'm paying Tyler a visit while you return the van." I stopped Matt's protest. "I'm still wearing the wire. If I don't talk to him, I won't know the best way to meet with Norma."

"Everything you want to do goes against everything I believe in as a detective."

"We have to think outside the box. Take off your cop hat."

"I'm back to work tomorrow, Stormi."

I doubted the case would be solved by then. The worst part of him going back to work was the fact I'd be a prisoner in my home. How creative could I be at finding ways to sneak out? "All the more reason to do as much today as possible."

He pulled the van into the spot assigned to Mom's store use and cut the engine. "We'll wait inside, eating something wonderful."

I landed a kiss on his lips and bolted from the van before he could change his mind. "I'll come get you when I know our next step."

The look on his face ranked on the thrill meter right above finding a spider in your salad. I hurried across the street.

Thankfully, Tyler wasn't waiting on customers. I spotted his dark head by the counter where customers grabbed sugar and napkins. "Hey, Tyler."

"Miss Nelson." He refused to meet my eyes. "We heard you were poisoned by our coffee. Mom is devastated. How could that happen?"

"I'm sure it was an accident." I ducked to peer into his face. Tears shimmered under the black eyeliner. "Where's your mother now? Maybe I could pay her a visit, show her I'm all right?"

"She's at home writing." He filled the napkin dispenser. "Trying to be a writer like you and make some money."

There were easier ways of making money. Writing was hard work. "I'll head over there right now and put her mind at ease." I smiled. "What kind of dessert does she like?"

"She'll say nothing because she doesn't want to get fat, but she loves red velvet cake."

Perfect. I said goodbye and headed to Mom's shop, hoping she had something made with red velvet cake.

"Cupcakes are all I have," Mom stated the moment I walked through the door. "Take her two and sweeten her up. I'll go broke at this rate." She handed me a small white box with pink polka-dots.

"This is pretty."

"The package is as important as what is inside. A lot of my supply orders are starting to trickle in. I feel very official."

Matt and Mary Ann followed me to my car, Ryan having headed to work for a few hours. I didn't think Norma would mind too much having Matt around while I spoke with her, I still thought it important that I speak with her alone. "Park around the corner. I'll walk up."

"Be careful," Matt said. His eagerness to stay in

the car immediately set my internal radar twanging.

"What's up?" I frowned. "It isn't like you to let me go without some kind of attempt to change my mind."

"That woman makes my skin crawl." He shuddered.

I laughed. "She came on a little strong at the library, did she? Is my big bad detective afraid of a woman?"

"I am of that one."

I was still grinning as I approached the small white house. In foreclosure or not, Norma's pride of ownership showed in flowers and a white picket fence. If she were innocent, I hoped she would manage to save her home. Tyler deserved it, if nothing else. Poor kid, having a prostitute for a mother. I pressed the doorbell. Imagine what he would have to go through if his mother went to prison for two counts of attempted murder?

"Stormi Nelson!" Again, I found myself suffocated in the perfumed bosom of Norma. "How are you feeling?"

"I'm fine. Tyler told me you were concerned, so I thought it would be nice to pay you a visit." I held out the crushed box of cupcakes. "I brought you these."

She opened the flap. "Oh, my favorite! Come in."

Where Cheryl's house had been cluttered and dirty, Norma's, although lived in, was near spotless. A sofa and love seat, covered with furniture throws occupied the front room. Through an arched doorway, I spotted a kitchen and eating nook. On the kitchen table, mismatched chairs around it, rested a laptop. The home exuded a welcome feel. The tension in my shoulders dissipated.

"Sit." Norma waved me to a chair. "I've coffee on. It will go perfect with these." She removed the slightly crushed cupcakes from the box and set them on a piece of vintage china.

Nothing about the woman's home would alert anyone to her colorful, yet scanty, wardrobe. She handed me coffee, which I watched her make, then watched as she drank.

"I appreciate you relieving my worries." She set her cup down. "When I heard you had been poisoned and that they thought it was from our coffee—" She wiped the back of her hand across her eyes, smearing a thick trail of mascara.

"It wasn't the coffee. Who told you?" Still wary, I stared into my mug. Maybe I could pretend to sip and only eat the cupcake.

"Ms. Dillow. I went into the library the next day to check out a couple of books on, uh, positions, and everyone was talking about it."

"I accidentally ingested some oleander." I bit into the cupcake. "I heard you were a writer."

"Well, sort of. I take books from authors I love and turn them into erotica." She grinned. "Way more fun, and it pays good money. This is why I'm eagerly awaiting your next novel. You're one of three authors that I do this with."

I wasn't sure whether to be flattered or disgusted. While I wasn't a prude, I was raised with certain values and Christian morals. "How eagerly are you waiting for the next book, Norma?"

"What do you mean?" Her hand trembled, clattering the china coffee cup against its saucer.

"What lengths would you go to in order to have more writing material?"

"I'm not sure why you're asking me this, but if I needed more material, I'd read a new author." Her eyes narrowed. "You're treating me as if I'm being interrogated."

"I'm sorry. I've heard you're in the process of losing your home. Desperate times call for desperate measures." I picked at the crumbs on my plate. For a possible suspect, Norma didn't anger easily.

"There are plenty of ways of making money. I've probably done most of them." She took a gulp of coffee. "I don't know what you've heard, and while money is tight, I'm no longer going to lose my home, and I'm no longer a prostitute."

My head snapped up. "That's wonderful."

"I really thought we could be friends, Stormi. One writer to another, and all. But I feel as if you're accusing me of something." Her eyes glittered with unshed tears, dispelling any notion I had of her being my stalker.

I reached across the table and took her hand. "I'd love to be your friend. Maybe we can do lunch when I finish this book. I'm releasing it next week."

"You know what would be sweet?" Norma got up to refill her mug, dispelling any ideas I might have of mine being tampered with. "We should start a writer's group. Sarah Thompson would be interested, I know. There are probably others."

No doubt. I sighed. While the idea had merit, the last thing I needed was another obligation. What happened to staying happily at home and creating wonderful characters? Oh, yeah. My agent wanted me to get out more. "I'll let you know."

I said my goodbyes and left, taking my time heading around the corner to where Matt and Mary

Ann waited.

"Why the depressed look?" Matt opened the door for me. "That visit went very well."

"She's a nice woman." I clicked my seatbelt into place. "We're back to square one."

"No, we aren't. So far, Cheryl is the top suspect. We haven't talked to Ms. Dillow yet," Mary Ann said, patting my shoulder. "You wait. Eventually it will all fall into place."

"Hopefully not with a gun pointed at my head."

Matt took his place behind the wheel. "That was gutsy practically asking Norma outright whether she was the unsub, but it seemed to have closed that door. I don't think she's the one. What's the plan with the librarian?"

"I'm not sure yet." I faced him. "What if my stalker isn't Cheryl or Ms. Dillow? What if we're running in circles?"

"Then your stalker is smarter than I've given them credit." He pulled the car away from the curb. "Maybe tomorrow while you're at home, you and Mary Ann can make a list of why or why not these two women might or might not be the stalker. I'll also toss their names around at the station and see if anything comes to light."

It was a good plan. Not only that, but I intended to find out what secrets my neighbors held. My stalker could very well be one of them.

21

I still hadn't come up with a plan on confronting Ms. Dillow by the time we pulled into the library parking lot. I was a bit curious as to how she knew I'd been poisoned. Maybe I could use that to my advantage.

This time, Matt accompanied Mary Ann and I. Ms. Dillow wasn't at her desk. While the other two pretended to browse for something to read, I went in search of the elusive librarian. I found her in the same conference room in which we'd held the meeting a few nights before. "Good afternoon, Ms. Dillow."

She stiffened. "I thought you were going to call me Janet. Friends call each other by their first names."

"My apologies." I glanced around the spotless room, now void of all decorations and poisonous flowers intended to kill me.

"I see you're suffering no ill effects from your illness." Her gaze flicked over me.

"I wasn't ill. I was poisoned. You know this, according to Cheryl Isaacson."

"That gossip mongrel. If you knew what was rumored that she had hidden in her house, you'd want nothing more to do with her." Ms. Dillow, Janet, moved past me and back to the main part of the library.

"I do know, and it's been taken care of." I

followed the woman's fast pace.

"Really?" She spun to face me, almost causing me to ram into her. "Then why is she still walking the streets? Seriously, the lack of law in this town … it's a disgrace."

"You seem to know an awful lot of what goes on around here."

"Of course I do. I'm the librarian. For now." She turned and stomped to the nonfiction side of the room.

I followed, motioning for Matt not to follow. What could happen in a sparsely populated library? I could see why the city was making cutbacks. "It's sad how people don't frequent the library anymore. Have you considered children's programs? Things to entice the young people?"

"Of course, I'm not an idiot." She grabbed an armful of books that weren't shelved and thrust them at me. "That's why I'm so excited when you release a new book. It brings people to the library. Why, we have a waiting list!"

Really? Glee bubbled up inside me like a carbonated drink.

"Why are you here, Stormi?"

"Oh." Come on, brain. Work fast. "Yeah. I need to book a room for the release party next week?"

"Next week?" She grinned. "I thought Cheryl was in charge of all that."

"We had a falling out, on account of what I found in her house."

Janet shrugged. "If the rumors are true, I still don't understand why she's walking the streets. People really do get away with murder around here."

"Do you have an empty room for next Friday evening?" I followed as she pulled books, added to the pile in my arms, and took from the pile to re-shelve.

"Of course. There's nothing else going on around here. Is there any chance I can get a sneak peek? Maybe I could come up with a creative way of advertising the fact."

"That's a wonderful idea." I'd give an advance copy to Cheryl, too. "It will be released in ebook form first, but print will follow soon after."

"That's strange, isn't it? The first book wasn't like that."

"But this is an in-between book." I grinned and shoved the books at her. "I'll call you next week to make final arrangements. See you on Friday." I fairly skipped from the building, waiting in the foyer for Matt and Mary Ann.

"That went well." Mary Ann hugged me. "One of our suspects actually gave us the prime idea that might draw them out of the woodwork. I'm going to play around with the cover a bit more, too. Make the killer on the front subtly more cartoonish."

Matt shook his head, leading the way to the car. "I'm surprised I don't have a head full of gray hair."

"You'd still be handsome." I ruffled his hair and raced away.

Pounding footsteps alerted me to the fact he followed. He grabbed me around the waist, swinging me in the air. I squealed as he nibbled my neck. I'd missed the carefree part of our relationship. Just when things had gotten good after Ms. Henley went off to jail, Matt had gone undercover. If life and death kept interfering we'd never get to take our relationship to a deeper level.

"You might want to cool it," Mary Ann said, motioning her head toward the glass doors of the library. "You have an audience."

I peered over Matt's shoulder to where Janet glared. If she was my stalker, I'd just reinforced in her mind exactly what my relationship with Matt was. "Let's go home."

He slid me down the length of his body, taking long enough to stir my blood and scramble my senses. "Let Mary Ann drive. Then we can neck in the back seat."

"Behave. My potential stalker is watching."

"Let her watch. It won't hurt for her to know that one of Oak Meadows' finest officers is looking out for you." He planted a kiss on my lips, then slid his arm around my waist. "Let me take you out to dinner tonight before I have to go back to the daily grind. Ryan can babysit my sister."

"Gee, thanks." Mary Ann punched his shoulder.

The prospect of a night out with my honey, not thinking of the case or my next book, filled me with happiness. I practically floated to my car. Until then, I hadn't noticed how much I needed a night off. Maybe Angela could lend me something pretty to wear.

Matt dropped Mary Ann and I off at the house, promising to return to pick me up in an hour. The day had flown by while visiting my three top suspects, and I was starved. So were my three babies. While rare for the two cats and the dog to be in the same room at the same time, dinner time was another thing altogether.

Serenaded with meows and whimpers, I filled food dishes and water dish, then headed upstairs to raid Angela's closet. She had more dating experience than I did; in fact, if dating were a college major, she'd have a Master's Degree. I flipped through her hangars, settling on a dress in royal blue. My red hair would contrast nicely with the color and the long sleeves would keep me from freezing to death when the temperatures dropped with the sun. I carried the dress, hangar and all, into my room.

The gentle beeping of the alarm alerted me that the rest of the family had returned. I turned on the water in the shower and waited for the temperature to adjust. While waiting, I checked my emails. I had one from my agent asking when the "bait" was going to be set out, and one from my stalker. I opened it and read, "Well played, my friend. I hope the little cup of poisoned coffee serves to remind you of who you're dealing with."

I had no idea who I was dealing with. That's why all the trickery and questions. I shut off my computer and headed for the shower.

Dressed, hair done and makeup on, I headed downstairs. Dakota held the freezer open, staring inside. "There's nothing to eat in this house."

"Where's your mother?"

"Out with that cop guy. The one who dumped her."

I pulled out a tray of mini-beef sliders. "Pop a few of these in the microwave for a minute and you're ready to go."

"You look hot. Where are you going?"

"Out with Matt. Mary Ann is here somewhere."

"Living room. She's agreed to watch an action movie with me. Cherokee is holed up in her room fighting on the phone with some guy. My mom and sister have the worst luck in men."

I gave him a side hug. "That's because they aren't picking men like you."

He blushed. "Have fun with Matt. He's cool."

Car lights shined through the window. "Yeah, I like him, too. See you later."

I bypassed Ryan on the way in as I headed out. "They're watching a movie right up your alley."

"Great." He headed straight for the kitchen. "Something smells good."

I smiled and shook my head, thankful there were at least twenty sliders on the tray I'd given Dakota. I needed to spend some more time in cooking therapy just to keep that big man happy. Once upon a time, I'd spent time cooking casseroles as a way to relax, but threats against my life had taken away that simple pleasure. I promised myself I'd cook all day tomorrow.

"You're smokin'." Matt held the car door open.

"You don't look so bad yourself." I noted the dark turtleneck and blazer which set off his blond hair. Of course the man could make a gunny sack look good. "Where are we going?"

"How does steak sound?"

"Wonderful." Other than a few bites of a cupcake, I hadn't eaten since breakfast.

We drove to Bart's Beef, way nicer than it sounded. Inside, the restaurant looked like an old time western bar and served the finest beef east, or west, of the Mississippi River. Not that I'd eaten in that many places, but I'd still be willing to bet on it.

Matt asked for a table near the window that overlooked a small pond. Romantic. Maybe someday he'd take me there for a proposal. I ducked my head to hide a smile and spread my napkin in my lap. Six months wasn't long enough to think of marriage, but at twenty-eight years old, I felt as if time was running out, and it wouldn't be a hardship waking up next to Matt every morning.

"Thank you for inviting me." I twirled my water glass. "I needed the distraction."

"I think we both do." He grabbed my free hand. "I've enjoyed being around you all the time. I'll miss you when I return to work tomorrow."

"I'll miss you, too." While he struggled to solve other crimes, I'd be dwelling on my own case. Something had to crack soon. I gave myself a mental shake. No thinking of stalkers and murder. Not for a couple of hours, at least.

I ordered a filet mignon, deciding to skip the blue cheese crust I usually ordered. I was planning ahead, hoping for a night of heavy kissing when Matt took me home. He ordered a T-bone. While we waited for the waitress to bring our orders, we talked about everything under the sun except my stalker, Cheryl, or Ms. Dillow.

Still, something niggled at the back of my mind. Something I was missing. Maybe I was thinking about it too hard. If I relaxed, whatever the elusive fact was would present itself.

"Dakota said Angela was out with Wayne. Did you talk to him?" I straightened as the waitress brought us our salads.

"I did. He was stressed with work and didn't want her to see him barking at everyone." He stabbed a tomato. "Not a very good reason, but it seemed legit to him."

"I wish she'd find a good man. Someone like Ryan."

"Not many men better. Could she handle a bi-racial relationship?"

"Angela can handle anything in long pants." I grinned over the rim of my glass.

He chuckled. "I suppose she probably can."

I glanced out the window, marveling at the moonlight on the pond. Sometimes, if a person were lucky, they could spot the swans gliding across the surface. Not tonight. Instead, the figure in the trench coat watched from the shadows. The person held a gun.

"Matt!"

He lunged across the table, dragging me from the booth and to the floor as the shot rang out. I grabbed my purse as the breath left my body.

22

We hit the floor in a shower of glass, sliding across the shards. Screams filled the air.

"Stay down! Stay here." Matt pushed against my shoulder, getting to his feet.

Oh, no, he wasn't. If he planned on going after the shooter, I had no intentions of staying behind. I struggled to my feet, doing my best to ignore the pain in my hands and knees. I'd worry about the damage to my body parts later.

I sprinted after Matt, who shoved through the back door of the restaurant. I hadn't known he'd brought his gun along, but seeing it clutched in his hand brought to my mind a measure of safety. I dug my pink nine millimeter out of my purse. I was beginning to wish it were Ms. Henley after me again. Except for the end, when I'd stumbled across her being the murderer, she'd basically left me alone. This person dogged my every step.

"I should have known you wouldn't listen." Matt grabbed me and yanked me behind a bush.

"Careful." I winced. "I think I have enough glass poking in me to rival a porcupine." I spotted a spreading stain on his bicep. "You're bleeding!"

"Hush." He parted the branches. "I've lost 'em."

I scanned the darkness as sirens wailed in the distance. If the shooter ditched the trench coat, he or she could be any one of the people converging on the scene. "I think they're gone."

"I agree. Stay down and follow me." Matt took my hand and we moved, using the bushes as coverage, toward the first patrol car to arrive.

After handing me into the care of the paramedics, Matt pulled out his cell phone and called Ryan. I wished he would let the medics take a look at his arm before he turned all detective. If his wound hurt as much as the multiple pricks from cuts all over my arms and legs, he had to be in pain.

I glanced at my knee as the medic pulled a rather large sliver of glass from my skin. Angela's once beautiful dress was stained with my blood. Multiple rips left the hem in tatters. I didn't need to worry about my stalker, my sister would kill me herself. I hissed as the medic sprayed antiseptic on my cuts. None of them seemed too serious, other than the one above my knee, which would require stitches.

Another medic cut away Matt's sleeve, revealing a nice little hole in his upper arm. My eyes widened right before I keeled over backward, striking my head on the door of the ambulance.

I must not have been unconscious for long since I woke to find myself still in the parking lot of the restaurant. I stared up into the worried face of Matt. "Sorry," I said. "I guess I haven't quite gotten used to blood, especially mine."

He laughed. "You should be by now." He cupped my face with one hand, his left arm being in a sling, and kissed me. "I'm fine. The bullet went all the way through. They've patched me up and given me a heavy dose of antibiotics. Other than being sore for a while, I'll live. You'll be tender for a few days yourself."

"I'm glad you're sticking around. I've grown quite fond of you." I hadn't thought of myself at all when spotting the shooter's gun. If Matt hadn't gone across the table first, I would have done the same for him. Now, he carried a bullet hole in his sculpted arm. I wanted to strangle the person responsible.

"I'm done here," the paramedic said. "Do you want a ride to the hospital for your stitches?"

I glanced at Matt, who shook his head. "I'll drive us there," he said.

"I wouldn't advise it, sir. You're running on adrenaline right now, but when that wears off, you shouldn't be behind the wheel of a car."

"I can drive." I hopped off the end of the ambulance and gasped at the pain in my leg.

"I'll take care of them." Ryan stepped around the side of the vehicle and scooped me in his arms. "Steele, you ready?"

"Yep." Matt thanked the paramedic and followed as Ryan's long strides carried me quickly to his car. He set me gently into the back seat before opening the door for Matt.

It might be against protocol, and the paramedics were probably deferring to Matt being a detective by allowing us to leave, but I was glad not to have an ambulance ride. Authors weren't known for having good medical insurance. I rested my head against the seat back and closed my eyes, suddenly feeling every one of the glass cuts.

"I've called your family," Ryan said. "They'll meet us at the hospital."

Wonderful. One more worry for Mom. She must

be regretting moving in with me by now.

Sure enough, the whole family met us outside the Emergency Room doors. I sighed and waited for Ryan to fetch a wheelchair, not wanting him to carry me in front of my sister. I still held out hopes the two would get together someday. I slid from the car and leaned against the side until he helped me into the chair.

"Is that my new dress?" Angela scowled as Ryan wheeled me past. "It's ruined. You owe me eighty-five dollars."

"Fine. I wanted something nice for my date, and you've seen my closet. It isn't like I expected any of this to happen."

"You never do." She tottered on high heels alongside of us, the black pencil skirt she wore making long strides impossible. She resembled some kind of crippled stork. How could anyone think that was sexy?

"Now is not the time," Mom said, taking the wheelchair from Ryan who went ahead to open the doors. "My baby is injured."

"This isn't a rare occurrence, Mom!" Angela continued to trot beside us.

"Maybe not, but she's in pain. I can see it in her face. Matt, are you okay?"

"He's been shot, Mom," I said, tears clogging my throat. Yes, I was in pain, but the fear of something happening to Matt overshadowed that.

"Gracious." Mom let go of the wheelchair and rushed to his side. "Let me help you."

I sat in the chair while the rest of my family hurried into the hospital. Seriously? "Hello?"

"I really wish you had respect for my things," Angela said, not skipping a beat as she hurried back to wheel me inside. "It's always been this way. Since you were little, you've messed with my clothes or toys."

"You've never minded before."

"You haven't ruined anything before."

"Point taken." I should have asked before borrowing the dress.

Matt and I, escorted by Ryan, were immediately led by a nurse to a private room with two beds. I was helped into one and Matt the other. From the firm set of his lips and the paleness of his usually tanned skin, I could tell the adrenaline was wearing off and pain setting in. I avoided glancing at his arm while a doctor patched him up and instead, concentrated on the stitches going into my knee and who knew I was having dinner with Matt that evening. I couldn't think of anyone outside of my family and Ryan.

Mary Ann and Dakota had watched a movie with Ryan. Angela had been on a date. Dakota was the only one I'd told about going out with Matt, and I hadn't told him exactly where we were going, although in a town the size of Oak Meadows, it wasn't hard to figure out. Cherokee had been on the phone. With a boy, Dakota had said. What boy and where had he been during the conversation? As far out there as it seemed, the only lead I had was my niece's phone call.

After having my knee stitched, my cuts cleaned for the second time, and Matt's gunshot taken care of, we were both given pain medicine and sent home. I wanted to wait before taking one of the white pills, but when your body is on fire from millions of tiny cuts, sometimes you have to give in.

Thirty minutes later, I was in my pajamas on the sofa feeling warm and fuzzy beside Matt. My family sat around us, watching us as if we were going to die on them at any moment. Mary Ann, after seeing that we were all right, had headed to bed.

"What?" I asked.

"We're worried about you." Mom folded her hands in her lap. "You've been injured and yet you sit there with a maniacal grin on your face. It isn't natural."

"That would be the pain meds, Mom." I giggled. "But I do have a question for Cherokee. Who was the boy you were talking to on the phone when I left?"

"Skip. Why?"

"Skip?" His name struck me as funny and my giggles increased.

Matt looked at me in alarm, then laughed along with me. Oh, Lord, don't let the shooter come after us now. We were as defenseless as a couple of mental patients.

"Where was he when you talked to him?"

"The park." She drew the words out slowly, as if by doing so I could understand her language. "By the library."

"Ah ha!" I finger stabbed the sky. "Ms. Dillow is my stalker. It's elementary, my dear Mr. Watson."

"Don't accuse people without proof." Ryan handed me a bottle of water. "I think you need to dilute your meds."

"It makes sense." I fumbled with the bottle cap, finally unscrewing it and dumping half the water in my lap. "Now it looks like I wet myself."

"Makes sense how, honey?" Mom took the bottle from me.

"The boy, Chip, was by the library. Ms. Dillow works at the library." Why couldn't they see this? "It was Ms. Dillow, in the library, with the revolver." I laughed so hard I fell over and almost rolled off the sofa. "It's simple deductive reasoning."

"Makes sense to me." Matt upended a water bottle of his own, except most of his made it in his mouth. "Ryan?"

"My boyfriend's name is Skip." Cherokee stormed from the room.

"I'll check into it," Ryan said. "See whether the librarian has an alibi. I'll question Cheryl, too. Word around town is that she's plenty upset with Stormi and plans to get even for Stormi ruining her life."

Killing me would definitely have ruined my life. "Check the closets of everyone in town. Someone owns that trench coat."

"Sure thing." Ryan grinned. "Anything else?"

I sat up, clutching a sofa pillow to my stomach and chewed the inside of my cheek. "No ... I think that's it. Things are a bit fuzzy right now. Matt, did you notice anything about the shooter?"

"They had a gun."

"I'm being serious." I hit him with the pillow.

"They wore a trench coat, a hat like Dick Tracy would wear, pulled low over their eyes, and gym shoes. Whoever it was could run, and they knew the layout of the area around the lake. It could be anyone."

"I should be on the force. I noticed the same things you did. With your training, you should have noticed something else. Don't beat yourself up that they out ran you. They had a big head start."

"I was kind of busy covering you." He wiggled his eyebrows. "Which was nice, by the way. You're soft."

"For Pete's sake." Mom stood. "The two of you are being ridiculous. Matt, I'll fix you a bed on the sofa. Stormi, upstairs." She pointed that way. "You need your rest. It's been a long day."

"Yes, Mom." I stood a bit unsteadily and made my way up the stairs where Sadie waited for me behind the closed bedroom door. "Oh, honey, I'm so sorry. I didn't mean to lock you in here. It's freezing." I must have closed her in after changing from out of Angela's dress. I went to pull down my covers.

My hand froze halfway to the quilt covering my bed. On my pillow was a single sheet of copy paper. Typed in a large font were the words, "Next time I won't miss. Finish the book!"

23

"Matt!"

Thundering feet told me of his and Ryan's approach. I pointed at the note when they barged into the room, hoping they would be able to lift fingerprints. We were way overdue for a break.

"Sadie was locked in here. That's why she didn't bark. Whoever was here, is someone she doesn't feel is a threat." I rushed to the window.

Ryan pushed me out of the way. "Stay back." He parted the curtains, showing the open window.

Some of the fuzziness from the pain meds flew out the open window. To climb inside, a person would have to use a ladder or the tree. To use the tree would require strength and athletic skill. I peered under Ryan's arm to see a ladder propped against the house. "Does that belong to Mark Wood? He was going to bring one by, remember?"

"I'll add him to the list of people to interview." Ryan pushed the ladder away from the house and closed the window.

"It's time to consider staying somewhere else for a while." Matt lowered himself to a sitting position on the bed. "This person is not afraid to enter the house, even with two detectives on the premises.

The lights flickered on in the Salazar's house. Had they just gotten home? Maybe after being in my house? Everyone was a suspect in my eyes.

"I don't want to leave my home. Why wasn't the alarm set?"

"We must not have set it when we rushed to the hospital." Mom glared at me, then flicked her gaze to Matt.

"Or when we returned," I said. "Unless the person came in when we were at the hospital. It's possible I didn't notice the note when I changed clothes." In fact, I'd headed straight to the bathroom upon arriving home and hadn't glanced at the bed.

Relieved that Sadie hadn't been locked in my room with a potential murderer, I sat next to Matt. After all, even my scaredy-cat-of-a-dog would have at least barked at an intruder before she hid under the bed. "Is there such a thing as an automatic alarm system? I think my family needs one."

"It should never be turned off." Matt shook his head.

"One of you needs to get off the bed," Mom said. "It isn't proper."

I shook my head, choosing to ignore her. With her and Ryan in the room, nothing improper could possibly happen even if Matt and I were so inclined, which we weren't. He respected my morals. Besides, I could barely hold my eyes open. "I really need to get some sleep."

"I'll check the house, set the alarm, and spend the night on one of the chairs in the living room," Ryan said. "I have a feeling once Matt closes his eyes, he'll be out for the count."

"That's for sure. I'm beat." Matt planted a

tender kiss on my forehead and reached out for Ryan to help him to his feet.

"I've a cot you can sleep on. It's got to be better than the chair. Come down to the basement with me." Mom slipped her arm through his. "After all this excitement, I'm too nervous to go down there alone."

They passed through my sister and her children who watched the proceedings from the doorway. Angela placed her arms around her children's shoulders. "We're all sleeping together tonight. Tomorrow, we're going to a hotel."

"Gross." Cherokee pulled away. "I can't sleep in the same bed as my brother. People will think we're some kind of freaks."

"We are." I slid under my thick quilt and closed my eyes.

When I opened my eyes the next morning, the October sun streamed through open curtains. Sadie slumbered peacefully on the bed beside me, reassuring me that Mom must have come in and opened the curtains. The delicious aromas of perking coffee and frying bacon drifted up the stairs and through my open door. I couldn't remember the last time I'd slept until … I glanced at the clock. Nine a.m.!

Half the day was gone. I jumped from bed, my knee reminding me in a very unpleasant manner that it was stitched, and rummaged through my closet for something to wear. I still had two chapters to write on the novella. If I slept too much, it wouldn't be ready for my suspects, uh, advance readers.

I dressed in yoga pants and another long-sleeved tee-shirt, my winter clothes of choice, then leaned over the banister. "Will someone bring me some coffee, please? I need to work." I should finish by the end of the day.

"I'm way ahead of you." Mary Ann carried a tray into my office. "Matt and Ryan are busy plotting out the best way to get our suspects to spill their guts. Your mother has gone to work, confident in Greta's ability to protect her. Your niece and nephew are staying home, at Angela's request, and she has grumpily headed to work." She set the tray on the end of my desk. "Wait until you see the latest version of the book cover. It's definitely going to set someone's temper to flaring."

"Good." I snatched a slice of bacon. "Injuries and near death are becoming too common in this family. We need to end this."

With my coffee and breakfast close at hand, I settled down to writing the last five thousand words of what was guaranteed to be a best seller. I might have planned on the novella being trash to coerce a killer out of hiding, but it had turned into something wonderfully thrilling. The perfect in-between story for two books.

"How are you going to get Cheryl's copy to her if she's making open threats against you?" Mary Ann sat in the only other chair in my office, a striped sateen castoff of my mother's.

"I haven't figured that part out yet. Maybe I'll just leave it on her porch." I hunched over my keyboard, letting my fingers fly.

Four hours later, I typed The End and printed off two copies. I clapped my hands and spun in my chair. I was ready to deliver and watch the fireworks.

"We can't go anywhere," Mary Ann informed me, glancing up from her laptop. "The men are gone interrogating the suspects."

"Then we'll go without them." I couldn't wait. Not now. I'd worked too hard for this. "I've got a gun and a Taser. We'll be perfectly safe."

"I bought a gun, too." Mary Ann showed me the cutest little twenty-two pistol. "I've never shot it, and hope I never have to, but I've got it, just in case."

"Then let's go." I jumped to my feet, my knee instantly reminding me to take things slow, and grabbed the printed copies and my purse. "We have to stop and have these bound. I know they won't look like a real book, but since I'm releasing it in ebook form at first anyway, it'll be good enough for its purpose."

"I'm excited to see this all finally coming to a close."

"Me, too." I gave her a serious look. "Things could get really dangerous now. We have to be cautious."

"Call me Cautious Cathy." She slung her purse over her shoulder and followed me out the door.

After making sure the pets were inside, and the two teenagers knew not to leave the house, Mary Ann and I headed for the nearest printer. Thirty minutes later, with two glossy copies of the novella, we went to Cheryl's house. Mary Ann texted Matthew, telling him of our plans, and ignored the texts he sent demanding we return immediately to the house. We would both deal with him later.

Cheryl's house still looked vacant. I pulled into the drive and cut the ignition. "Should we knock?"

Mary Ann shook her head. "I can't go in there again. I'll throw up."

"Matt said it had been cleaned."

"Unless they ripped up carpet, bleached everything, and painted, it isn't clean enough for me."

She was right, making me doubly glad that Rose was safely in a lovely nursing home where people would actually make an effort to keep her company. I planned on paying her a visit as soon as my stalker was behind bars. "I'll leave the book propped against the door. She won't be able to miss it."

I left the car door open in case I needed to get away fast and limped to the porch. Partially open curtains showed that the house had indeed been emptied of all but the barest of necessities. I doubted the sofa against the wall was new, but if Cheryl didn't mind sitting on it, why should I complain? I leaned the envelope containing the book against her door and hobbled back to the car.

"Is she home?" Mary Ann asked.

"I don't know." I honked to attract her attention if she was home and backed onto the road. "Next stop, the library." Mary Ann's phone buzzed.

"My brother has been texting and/or calling every minute. I'm more afraid of going home to see him than facing a murderer."

I didn't fault her there. "We'll be fine. We're almost finished and haven't been gone an hour yet. Tell him to stop overreacting." My cell phone rang. I glanced at Mary Ann. "Is he mad or are we in danger that we don't know about?"

"From his messages, I'd say he's mad."

I bit the inside of my cheek, deciding to answer my phone. "Hey."

"What are you doing?"

"Heading to the library to drop off a copy of the finished book. Didn't Mary Ann tell you?"

"Of course she told me! Why couldn't it wait until I got back? Ryan and I are sitting here and you and my sister are gone."

"We'll be home in fifteen minutes. Twenty tops.

I promise. Bye." I hung up and grinned. "That wasn't too bad."

"Wait until we get back," she laughed.

At the library, we approached the front desk and inquired as to whether Ms. Dillow was working. The girl said she was in the supply room at the back. We headed that way, meeting her halfway. "Janet." I smiled. "Here is the completed book. I thought you might like to read it before the release party next week."

"Really? You've finished?" Her eyes narrowed. "Is this a complete book or that silly novella you talked about?"

"The novella. It should satisfy my readers until I finish the next full length. I hope you enjoy it. See you next Friday." I turned, grabbed Mary Ann's arm, and limped back to the car. "Now, we wait."

"You should be able to tell by any other emails you receive whether the stalker is Cheryl or Ms. Dillow."

"Oh, it's one of them all right." All an email would do was let me know whether my plan was working or not.

We made a quick stop by Mom's store, purchased a cake to sweeten the moods of the two men waiting at the house, and then hurried home. Matt and Ryan were at the kitchen table, obviously waiting to pounce if I was one minute late.

Matt glanced at the clock on the microwave. "Very good. Nineteen minutes."

I set the cake on the table and went to grab plates. "I'm sorry for leaving, but I needed to get those copies delivered. The whole case could be resting on these two women's responses. Now, we sit back and wait. If nothing happens before the release party, and the party goes by without a hitch, then I've been wrong this whole time and we start over."

"Leaving without telling us cannot keep happening." Matt cut the cake.

"We did tell you."

"After you had already left." He handed me a piece of rainbow cake with cream cheese frosting. "I don't mean to be heavy handed, Stormi, but recklessness might guarantee you don't live long enough to attend your release party.

"We weren't reckless. We planned every step of today and were perfectly safe every minute."

"Tell that to the person trying to kill you."

24

A week passed with no sign or word from my stalker, Cheryl, or Janet. Matt and Ryan were as confused as I was.

I secured my hair into a French twist, then stepped back from the mirror. The black slacks and long-sleeved crimson blouse seemed the epitome of a mystery writer. A dash of scarlet lipstick and I was ready to head to my book release party.

Mom had already left. Greta and she were in charge of the refreshments, and Angela, fearing tonight would be the night my snooping finally did me in, had opted to stay home with her children. I couldn't blame her. Apprehension sloshed through my veins. Either the novella had satisfied my stalker or tonight was *the* night; The night it all came to a showdown.

"We're going to be late," Mary Ann called up the stairs. "You should be the first one there to greet your fans."

She really took her job as my assistant seriously. It was like having another mother. "I'm coming."

"You look great." Matt greeted me with a kiss on the cheek and opened the front door. "I'll go out first. The alarm is set. You stay behind me all the way to the car. At the library, I'll exit first and you follow closely into the building. Ryan is already there, making sure everything is safe."

I nodded, slung my purse over my shoulder, comforted by the weight of my gun as my purse swung against my side. While I might usually balk at someone telling me what to do, this time I agreed to follow his orders. After being shot at through the restaurant window, I hadn't left the house other than delivering the reader copies to my suspects. I was finished tempting fate. Almost. I'd be finished after my stalker was caught. I promised.

We made the drive to the library in silence and formed our tight formation as we marched inside. Mom immediately handed me a tall blended mocha coffee. "Don't worry. It hasn't left my sight."

Where were my suspects? The party was due to start in forty-five minutes. Instead of a conference room, Janet had received permission to close the library at five and reopen at seven for the party. She seemed to be expecting a large crowd. I hoped so, for the library's sake. It pained me to think the beautiful historic brick building might have to close due to budget cuts. Maybe I could make a large donation to the library to prevent that from happening.

"Stormi Nelson!" Cheryl raced toward me, knocking Mary Ann out of the way.

Matt stepped in front of me, one hand on the gun in his shoulder holster. "That's close enough."

She glared and waved the copy of A Killer Plot in my face. "What is this?"

"That's my newest release. I told you that." I tried to appear unshaken and sip my drink. Instead, my legs grew weak and my hands trembled.

"I don't know what this is, but it can't be your

newest release!" She threw it at me. "First, you ruin my life by butting in and taking my mother away, now you've written drivel that I can't possibly sell.

"I thought it was actually quite good."

She shrugged. "It is, but it is so different from your first book, it's almost as if someone else wrote it." She gripped her hair with both hands and pulled so hard I thought she'd rip the auburn strands from her head. "What am I supposed to do with you?" She reached around Matt and pinched me.

"Ow!" I slapped at her hand.

She tried to hit me back.

I slammed my cup on her fingers, not that the plastic cup did much damage other than make her more angry.

"You need to leave before I slap cuffs on you," Matt said, taking a step forward.

"This isn't the end, Stormi. Not by a long shot." She stormed away, knocking into Janet, who dropped an armload of books.

Janet stared after her for a moment, then glanced at the copy of my manuscript on the floor. "I guess she didn't like your book."

"Did you?"

Before she could answer, someone called to her from the back of the room. "Someone needs to pick these up. They go on the fiction cart." She pointed at the dropped books and hurried away.

A teenage girl darted forward, scooped up the books, and left as fast as she'd appeared. I felt as if I'd stepped into Alice's wonderland with the way people flitted around me. I headed to the table which displayed a large poster size picture of my book's cover.

Mary Ann had really outdone herself. The cover

still didn't have the whimsical look of my first book, but it suited the novella perfectly. My outfit matched the colors, adding to the theme. All we needed was a plump suspect carrying a too-large knife. My stalker couldn't help but be annoyed at the way we had portrayed him or her.

As more people arrived, Matt stayed closer to my side than ever. I felt like recently separated Siamese twins who couldn't get used to the fact they were no longer joined. "I don't like this," he said. "Not one bit."

"What could possibly go wrong with you here?" Of course, his presence would deter anyone from making an attempt on my life, which kind of defeated the purpose of antagonizing my stalker. If he couldn't get close, I couldn't figure out who he was.

I sighed and concentrated on watching the crowd for anyone who seemed too interested in me. My ego took quite a hit as few of the arriving patrons bothered to glance my way. Why did they come if they weren't fans who wanted to meet me? "You're scaring away my readers."

"Too bad." Matt shrugged. "Your safety is more important than gushing fans."

"Not really. Those fans are my bread and butter." I set my cup on the table and plopped into a nearby chair. If Matt continued to hover, my plans could all be for naught. What I needed was a distraction.

I pasted on a smile as a woman with two small children approached the table. "Good evening."

"Is the book out?"

"It's available as an ebook. It will be released in paperback in six months."

She frowned. "I don't have an ereader." She left.

She wouldn't be the only one. A lot of folks who frequented libraries preferred the feel of a book in their hands. Usually, that would prompt me to find a solution, but tonight, the focus wasn't about getting the book into as many hands as possible. It was about finding a potential killer.

"Could you at least stand a few feet away and smile?" I frowned at Matt. "You look like a disgruntled bodyguard."

"I am." He took two steps to the side.

Ryan approached the table. "Where do you want me? I've been moving back and forth between the two entry doors, but that doesn't seem very efficient. Could we get away with locking one of them?"

"Do it. We'll put up a sign stating to use the other door. We want to funnel everyone through one door." Matt pulled out his cell phone, glanced at the time, and slid it back into his pocket. "Show time. It's seven o'clock. If the stalker isn't already here, they'll be arriving any minute."

Ryan left.

Or any time between then and nine o'clock, I thought. I sipped more of my drink. It was going to be a long night.

"The parking lot is full," Mary Ann said, dropping a stack of glossy photos of the book cover on the table. "I thought you could sign and hand these out to generate interest. I placed the rest of the box in the storage room. Ms. Dillow didn't want them cluttering up the space. She said she prides herself on a clean library." She rolled her eyes and strolled away.

"What a great idea!" I dug in my purse for my favorite signing pen, a pink and silver fountain pen with a smooth moving ball. I passed the next ten minutes signing my name across the lower corner of ten of the photos. Within five minutes, those ten were gone, and I'd started on another batch. Mary Ann was full of great ideas. I should have hired an assistant a long time ago.

Loud voices alerted me to Cheryl and Janet in the back of the library. Cheryl waved her arms around, her face red, until Janet put a hand on her shoulder and steered her out of sight. An uncontrollable urge to know what they argued about filled me.

"Don't even think about it," Matt said. "Stay right where you are."

"You're so mean." I kept signing. "I need to use the restroom. Are you going to follow me in there, too?"

"Take Greta with you and use the one in the library, not the foyer."

I guess he figured once a cop always a cop. I pushed to my feet, shook the pain out of my signing hand, and approached the refreshment table. "Greta, Matt said I have to take you with me to the restroom."

"Of course, you do, dear." She grabbed her purse. "Get your purse."

"Why?"

"You should never leave it unattended."

"Okay." I lengthened the word. People were strange creatures. My purse wasn't unattended, considering Matt still stood beside the table, but if I wanted to try and do some snooping, I'd do what she said. Hopefully, once in the restroom, she'd need to do some business and I could sneak out while she was in a stall.

I grabbed my purse and headed to the restroom. Darn. It contained one stall, unlike the one in the foyer which could accommodate five people. Now what? I slipped into the stall. I needed to think, which was difficult because Greta prattled on about how much she enjoyed working with my mother and how she thought she would never have the opportunity to make money doing what she loved.

It was no use. I'd have to come up with another plan. I flushed, still carrying on my ruse, and stepped out of the stall. "Your turn."

"Stay here, Stormi. I'll only be a minute." She slipped into the stall.

The minute I saw her pants pooled at her feet, I slipped out just in time to see Janet duck into the storage room.

Perfect. I could follow her on the pretense of fetching more fliers. I hitched my purse more securely on my shoulder and slipped in behind her.

Stacks of boxes filled the space. A few books lay on a table in preparation of being covered with clear book protectors and barcode labels. But where was Janet? She had only had a few seconds head start on me.

A thump sounded in the back of the room, then light flooded the small space. I headed in that direction as a back door slammed. The light in the room blinked off, plunging me into darkness. My little escapade had landed me in trouble. Why couldn't I listen to Matt?

Maybe there was a logical explanation. Maybe the light bulb burned out. Maybe Janet had left through the back door doing nothing more sinister than closing the door after her. The thump could have easily been a box falling over. I turned and put my hand out to try and find the door I'd entered through. It couldn't be far. I'd only taken a few steps inside.

Something skittered to my right. "Hello?" Why

did people in trouble say that as if they really expected an answer? I clamped my mouth shut. I didn't want to be one of those 'too stupid to live heroines' a person saw in a B horror movie. I took another step.

A flashlight blinded me. "Finally." Janet lowered the light. In her hand, she held a pistol aimed at my chest. "Out the back door, sweetie." She guided me past Cheryl lying in a pool of blood, and outside.

I never had the opportunity to reach for my gun.

25

Janet marched me across a small parking lot in the back designated for library employees and motioned for me to get behind the wheel of an older model Toyota. I glanced around, saw no one who could help me, and did as I was told. Too bad I didn't listen to Matt when I had the chance.

Unlike six months ago, this time the killer didn't take me from my home where I'd been minding my own business. Sort of. I'd actually gone next door to investigate a strange noise. This time, I was taken from a public place, right under Matt's nose.

Janet slipped me a piece of paper. "Go here."

"Can't you just give me directions?"

"I'd rather not speak with you right now." She poked me in the arm with the gun. "I'm annoyed."

"Did you kill Cheryl?"

"Probably. She was interfering with your job, which in turn affects my life. Drive. We have work to do."

Work meant she wasn't necessarily going to kill me, right? I followed the directions on the paper, taking us out of town and into the back country. Half an hour later, we pulled up in front of a mobile home beside the river. The dank odor of swamp and wet mud filled the air. "You live here?"

"Don't be ridiculous. I live in town. This is my family's hunting cabin. Get out and no funny business. I don't want to shoot you ... yet."

"You almost killed me at the restaurant."

"No, I didn't. I am a very good shot. If I had wanted to shoot you, I would have." She motioned for me to exit the vehicle. My heels sank several inches into swampy ooze. I grimaced and sloshed my way toward the trailer. "Wait, my purse." I turned to head back.

"You don't need it. Keep going."

Ugh. My gun was useless.

We entered a trailer containing nothing more than a dinette with mismatched chairs and a sagging sofa. On the table rested a laptop. My laptop.

"How did you get that?"

"I went to your house, told your niece you needed it for the party, and she gave it to me." She grinned like a shark. "You should really teach her not to be so trusting. Now write. You aren't leaving until you've written something I approve of."

"Write what?"

"Anything except the drivel you're trying to pass off as a book." She gave me a shove, then sat in a chair opposite the laptop. "I want you to write one where I am a poor misunderstood librarian trying to make a living."

I was right. It was about her moment of fame. "Wanting to be a character in a book doesn't warrant you killing Cheryl."

"That's your fault." Janet twirled the gun on the table. "If you hadn't upset her so badly, she wouldn't have felt the need to cause problems and get in my way."

"You cannot blame your twisted logic on me." I opened my laptop and immediately clicked on the internet browser. Darn it. No wifi. "I can't write while you're pointing a gun at me."

"You don't have a choice. Start with the first email I sent you and go from there. It should be an easy book to write."

Not likely. My fingers shook so badly I couldn't type a coherent word. Oh, Matt, I'm so sorry.

By now, the party was over and my family would be frantic. I'd hoped to send them a message via email, but Janet seemed to have thought of everything. I pulled up her first email and copied and pasted it into a document. She was right. It would make a great opening for a novel.

She got up from the table and opened a small refrigerator. Pulling out a beer, she popped the tab. I would have pictured her as a wine drinker, myself. "Do you have any water?"

"You can have a bottle of water after you've written three thousand words. Each chapter will get you a reward. Water, food, sleep, and so on."

She definitely ranked as one of the craziest people I'd ever had the misfortune of meeting. I glanced to my side and out a cracked window. There seemed to be only one way in and out of the property. She would see Matt coming a mile away.

"Why is this so important to you?" I lifted my fingers from the keyboard. "It can't be because I wrote my last book about Ms. Henley."

"It can be about anything I want it to be about." She guzzled her beer, then tossed the can on the floor. "I'm running the show."

"Is this because you're losing your job?"

"Partly. I've given most of my adult life to that library and now they want to cast me aside like an unwanted book. When you wrote that last mystery, people flocked to the library wanting a copy. I had a waiting list twenty people long. If you wouldn't take so long in between books, maybe the committee would reconsider."

"It's a bit late for that now, don't you think? I've seen you at church so you must be a believer. Why not let God handle the details of your future?" Not that her future was very undecided. She wouldn't have to worry about a roof over her head. She'd spend the next ten years or so in jail.

"Don't talk to me about God. I've spent my whole life serving Him and for what?"

She got another beer. Maybe if I kept her talking and drinking, I could overpower her and escape.

"Keep typing."

"I'm researching." I leaned back and crossed my arms. "I need to know how this story is going to end."

"It's going to end with you dead if you don't get to writing."

"If you're going to shoot me anyway, why should I bother writing?" Oh, Lord, don't let her shoot me. "I've also made the decision to give a large donation to the library to prevent it from closing. If you kill me, that won't happen."

"Write it down." She jumped up and pulled a notepad from a kitchen drawer. "Your last will and testament. Leave your money to the library. I'll be the one who finds your lifeless body lying across your suicide note. I'll be the hero."

Delusional was the word I'd use. "I'm not going to leave a suicide note. If you shoot me, the book won't get written and the money won't be donated. We're at a standoff, Janet. You can't win this." My heart threatened to beat free.

Her face darkened. I could almost see the wheels turning in her head. "Then there really isn't a reason to keep you here."

Not the reaction I expected. I bit the inside of my lip. "How about … since money seems to be your biggest motivator … we could be co-authors on this next book? We could split the royalties fifty-fifty, including the novella." Not that I expected it to really take place. After all, eventually she'd be arrested, right?

"That's an idea." She tapped her forefinger on the table top. "I am a library, and thus very well read, I would have a lot to contribute to the writing of a novel."

"Not to mention you've already given me the plot, and it's a killer."

"True. You'll have to change the title on that stupid novella. This book is *A Killer Plot*."

Her grin sent ants scurrying up my spine. Now that I looked at her more closely, it was clear that the hamster turning the wheel in her brain was dead.

I typed a few more words, jotting down her expression for future reference. This would be as big of a seller as *Anything For a Mystery*. Now that I knew how the last chapter played out, and how I hoped the story would end, the writing would flow quickly. I'd be done in a little under two months. I did not intend to spend that time locked in a rusty trailer beside a swamp.

Where was Matt? I stood, popping the kinks from my back, keeping my eyes glued on Janet. She narrowed her eyes and gripped the handle of her gun. I wish I had the fortitude to tackle her, even though she held a weapon. If I had my purse, we could have had an old-fashioned showdown.

I resumed my seat and started typing. As long as the sound of fingers hitting the keyboard filled the room, I would still breathe. I prayed as I typed, praying for protection, for wisdom, for Matt to show up with the cavalry, anything to get me out of there alive.

Two hours later, bladder screaming for release and mouth as dry as Arizona in the early summer, I showed Janet my word count. Three thousand and twenty-seven words. "Break time."

"You have fifteen minutes. Water is in the fridge. Next three thousand words and you can have five hours of sleep."

"Gee thanks. Where's the restroom?"

"Down the hall and to the left. The window is painted shut, so you can't get out that way."

I sighed and headed down the hall. Inside, I couldn't resist tugging on the window anyway. Sure enough, it wouldn't budge. But all was not lost. Sneaking up to the trailer was Matt and Ryan, accompanied by ten men in uniform. I knocked on the window to get their attention and waved. Matt gave me the okay signal.

I rushed to do my business, knowing that prolonging any longer would result in an embarrassing accident, then hurried back to the table where Janet stared out the window. "Well, now we know how this story is going to end." She turned the gun on me.

A shot rang out, taking her to the floor. I ran my hands over my body to make sure I hadn't been shot. Not finding any holes or feeling any pain, I leaped over her and dashed outside where Matt waited with open arms. Somewhere in the muck of the ground, I'd lost my stilettos. No worries. I'd buy another pair. Ryan and two police officers ran past us.

"Are you all right?" He ran his hands down my arms.

"I'm perfect." I slipped my arms around his waist and rested my cheek against his chest. "She just wanted me to write another book and save her job."

"She's still alive," Ryan called from the trailer. "Get a medic in here."

I closed my eyes, relieved the poor delusional woman wouldn't die. I would still donate to the library to keep it open. The town deserved to have a library. "Did you find Cheryl? Is she dead?"

"No, she's alive. Janet Dillow isn't a murderer."

"Not for lack of trying. How did you find me?"

"We put a tracker in your purse." He set me at arm's length and peered into my face. "I knew you'd figure out a way of ditching us."

He knew me so well, this handsome man of mine. I retrieved my purse from Janet's car, almost asking that he remove the tracker, then thought better of it. Who knew what the next few months would bring? I might find myself in the middle of another investigation where Matt needed to know where I was. There were worse things than being tracked by your detective boyfriend.

"I'm ready to go home," I said, slinging my purse over my arm. There were other questions I needed answers to, like how my neighbors knew each other, but those could wait until a later time. Maybe, they would form the plot of my third mystery.

"That's the best idea you've had in a long time. But first—" He lowered his head and claimed my lips. When we came up for air, he touched his forehead to mine. "I guess this is how our relationship is going to work, huh? You scaring years off my life, and me driving like a maniac to save you?"

"I'm pretty sure that's accurate." I pulled him down for another kiss.

The End

ABOUT THE AUTHOR

Multi-published and Best-Selling author Cynthia Hickey had three cozy mysteries and two novellas published through Barbour Publishing. Her first mystery, Fudge-Laced Felonies, won first place in the inspirational category of the Great Expectations contest in 2007. Her third cozy, Chocolate-Covered Crime, received a four-star review from Romantic Times. All three cozies have been re-released as ebooks through the MacGregor Literary Agency, along with a new cozy series, all of which stay in the top 50 of Amazon's ebooks for their genre. She has several historical romances releasing in 2013 and 2014 through Harlequin's Heartsong Presents. She is active on FB, twitter, and Goodreads. She lives in Arizona with her husband, one of their seven children, two dogs and two cats. She has five grandchildren who keep her busy and tell everyone they know that "Nana is a writer". Visit her website at www.cynthiahickey.com

39555655R00120

Made in the USA
Lexington, KY
27 February 2015